Quantum Death

A. G. Hayes
with Raymond Gaynor

Savant Books and Publications
Honolulu, HI, USA
2016

Published in the USA by Savant Books and Publications
2630 Kapiolani Blvd #1601
Honolulu, HI 96826
http://www.savantbooksandpublications.com

Printed in the USA

Edited by Daniel S. Janik
Cover Art "Quantum Computing" ID 49624820 © Nicholashan |
Dreamstime.com; Couple Woman Man Detective Secret Agent
Criminal Silhouette Photo © Pixattitude | Dreamstime.com
Cover Design by Daniel S. Janik

13-digit ISBN: 978-0-9963255-3-0

Dedication

To those who believe in in freedom, justice, democracy, and Koski and Falk.

Acknowledgements

I want to thank Raymond Gaynor for his brilliant ideas and all the hard work that went into QUANTUM DEATH. Thank's Ray, it's a joy working with you! Special thanks to Patricia Holmberg for pre-proofing the manuscript and helping seamlessly stitch together my and Ray's contributions.

G. Hayes

I was surprised when several ideas we each were discussing for a new political thriller suddenly came together in QUANTUM DEATH. Collaborating has been sheer delight. Another special thanks to Patricia Holmberg for her assistance helping smooth transitions between A. G. and my contributions.

Raymond Gaynor

Chapter 1

Susan Koski eased out of bed without making a sound. Joseph Falk never moved, the top of his head showing from beneath the covers assuring her he was fast asleep. Slowly she crept to the bedroom door, turned the knob…and the bedside phone rang.

"Damn it!" Her birthday surprise breakfast for Falk was ruined. She waited while Falk growled and snatched up the phone.

"Falk." Within seconds he was sitting on the edge of the bed wide awake, listening intently and waving for Koski to pick up the extension on the dressing table on the other side of the bed.

Koski immediately recognized the voice of their boss, Tom Stewart, head of Cerberus, America's ultra-secret "off the board" information and action agency.

"You on the line, Koski?" Stewart asked, continuing a

moment later, "Good. Now both of you listen up."

There was a soft click and the tone on the line changed. Both Koski and Falk knew what was coming was top secret. "We have a problem."

Koski looked across the bed, raised her eyebrows and mouthed the words…Happy Birthday.

Chapter 2

Earlier

"Something happened?"

"Yes. Tonight at oh-two-oh-sixteen hours, sir."

"Okay. What?" asked Tom Stewart, trying to shake off his grogginess, having been awakened from a deep sleep at four in the morning.

"That we don't exactly know, sir."

"What the hell does that mean: You don't 'exactly' know? What, then, do you know 'inexactly'?"

"We don't exactly know that either, sir."

"Then why are you waking me at this God-awful hour? It better be a significant 'something'!"

"That we do know."

"Go on…"

"At least we know it's *probably* significant, and…"

Stewart slid an arm into the sleeve of yesterday's rumpled

shirt, while trying to hold onto the receiver of the conventional phone he kept beside his bed, in the process becoming hopelessly entangled. "For God's sake! Cut to the chase, soldier!" he growled into the shirt-covered receiver.

"Sir! Tonight at oh-two-oh-sixteen hours, there was a pointed fluctuation in the internet, Sir!" The voice on the other end paused to allow Stewart time to absorb the importance of the message. Whatever significance it had, however, was totally lost on Stewart, who was busy untangling himself, repeatedly brushing away the offending phone cord while attempting to button the front of his shirt. "A 'fluctuation'…an *intentional* 'fluctuation'?" asked Stewart, his irritation growing by the second.

"Ah, well, Sir, no one actually detected the fluctuation, only its echo. A majority of our cyber-security guys, however, are certain it was intentional. The remainder aren't even sure it happened. It was the intensity of their debate that caught the Night Ops Officer's attention, and apparently caused him to 'push the button' so to speak, which requires me to call you."

"An echo? An *echo* of a *possible* flucuation in the internet? You woke me for something that might not even be real?"

"Who's to say what's real with the internet, Sir. But you see the dilemma, I hope. Given these times, if it is real, it's unique and quite likely intentional. And it's something we've never before seen with which we presumably have no experience. Our counterparts, the senior cyber-analysts at NSA, are already calling it a 'singularity,' and the implications of that, well…"

"Alright, alright. So you called me as required. What else can you tell me about this 'echo of an intentional fluctuation'?" Stewart asked shaking his lower body into last night's pants while attempting to grasp the tab of the fly and hold the phone in the crook of his neck at the same time. The visual impression, if anyone had been watching, would have been that of a failing contortionist.

"Our cyber experts have shifted from talking their recognizable, but normally indecipherable 'computerese' to what the Night Ops Officer is calling 'real quantum gibberish'. Physics stuff. Like, some are calling this unobserved event a digital 'big bang,' you know, like the big Big Bang. The beginning of the cosmos. Except this one wasn't really that big or that bangish from what I could catch."

"'Bang'?" repeated Stewart, slipping on his favorite London Fog coat and one of his many fedora hats while searching about for his car keys. "You say something went 'bang'?"

"Well, 'bangish' as far as anyone can say regarding a digital event, reserving a real 'Bang' for the Big Cosmic One. The unsettling part is hearing them use the two increasingly interchangeably. I overheard one of the more understandable experts call it a 'multi-dimensional quantum ripple in space-time fabric'. That's when Mister Rellin, the Night Ops Officer, ordered me to call you, Sir. To be honest, it's total chaos over here."

"I can hear the shouting in the background over the phone. But why call me? Why not first call…"

"Mister Relin told me to tell you that one theory—he stressed the word 'theory'—is that while no one observed the actual event, 'echo-ripples' from it appear to be expanding out in every direction from a specific geographic point, and, while most of them don't appear to be doing anything in particular, a few have been reported to have caused byte-changes in nearby computers. For example, a few minutes ago, a 'ripple-edge' passed over and apparently interacted with a supposedly secure nuclear-missile launch site. The Launch Officer said it didn't initiate a launch sequence, or shut down the facility, or cause any permanent damage that they could ascertain, but the targeting sequences for two of the missiles were scrambled, making them temporarily inactive. Mister Rellin said to stress to you that, so far, these are the only two intercontinental ballistic missile targeting sequences we know of that were changed, and the targeting code, in each case, automatically reverted back after the 'echo-ripple' passed and their internal computers rebooted. He also said to stress that the change, if it had happened during an actual launch crisis, would, at best, have made the missiles miss their assigned targets, and at worst caused them to detonate in their silos."

"Okay. That's more than serious enough to justify waking me. Tell Mister Rellin I'm on my way," Stewart yelled into the phone while heading for the door of his Washington DC apartment. The phone line abruptly snapped taut, issuing a vibratory warning.

"Ah, that's not all, Sir," the voice from the receiver end continued.

Stewart stopped dead, took two steps back and returned the landline receiver to his ear. "Yes…?"

"Well, again there's disagreement about this, but there's some, like I said, who think that the 'event' itself, although not observed, may be significant. It appears to have lasted less than a hundredth of a millisecond, but *while* it happened, it looks like for the briefest moment an unusual transmission link of some kind was established with, of all places, Laplacia, Vermont—that's a very small town outside Battleboro on the way to Marlboro, which is…"

"I know where Battleboro, Vermont, is! Finish what you were saying about the transmission link, man. What more can you tell me about this?"

"Yes, well, it appears that for an instant—we're talking less than the duration of the event—something in Laplacia self-actuated, then, immediately after, disappeared."

"What?"

"Just a moment, Sir. Mister Rellin's conveying more information he wants me to pass on. It is possible—no, Mister Rellin says it's now 'likely', Sir—that some kind of separate internet 'transaction' also occurred *immediately after* that. We've no idea what kind of transaction, but preliminary information suggest that someone—or 'someones'—were sending bids ostensibly for the purchase of the Eastern seaboard of the US. This could represent a second type of 'event', Sir."

"What the hell? Is this for real?"

"None of it makes sense to me, Mister Stewart. I'm only the messenger, and Mister Rellin's trying his best to summarize what the geniuses here are guessing based on multiple ongoing inter-agency analyses of the originally undetected event. Mister Rellin says now that there's little question among the group that this event—they're all officially calling it an 'event' rather than a 'bang' now—is undoubtedly more significant than our current interpretation. The event, he says, is similar to…no, now they're saying it *is*…a 'quantum event'. Sir, you've got to get here. Some think this may be the beginning of a new kind of cyber-attack against the United States, and whoever's behind it is screwing with the very fabric of space-time. Our analysts are talking things like 'targets' and 'side-effects', like creating parallel worlds, with further effects and outcomes that could threaten our very physical existence. One expert is claiming it has already changed our future 'timeline'. I mean, Jesus, Sir...!"

Stewart checked the clock on the wall. It was already oh-six-hundred hours. He tossed the land phone, fished his cell phone out of his pants pocket, and speed-dialed his two best field agents.

"Falk," a sleepy voice on the other end said.

"This is 'Father'. You on the line, Koski? Good, now both of you listen up: We have a problem. Get your asses down to the Cerebrus situation room. Now!"

Chapter 3

Susan Koski and Joseph Falk joined Stewart just outside the Cerebrus situation room inside one of a row of nondescript greystone buildings lining a nondescript street in the Washington DC suburbs. The unobtrusive brown door looked exactly like that of all the other houses, belying no indication of the frenetic activity inside.

During the time it took the three to arrive, it had become irritatingly clearer to the night shift denizens that some kind of event and bidding had indeed occurred—a bidding, as the liaison officer had indicated over the phone, resulting in what appeared to be purchase, and, by implication, possession and control by "persons unknown" of the United States Eastern Seaboard. Whether the 'event' and 'auction' were separate, or two aspects of an integrated, more sinister action, no one was yet willing to volunteer.

Koski and Falk followed Stewart up five rows of steps, and,

after providing the required identification to the audiovisual box beside the door, slipped in, passed a couple of armed military hallway guards, and through one of many unlabelled doors. Inside the room, everything was, as the liaison officer had indicated, total chaos.

The huge room, usually outfitted in largesse "boardroom" style, and sporting all the latest in digital information communication technology on one wall, had been organically subdivided along it's perimeter into fifty or more makeshift, working command and control centers, each with a Cerebrus representative, military liaison, security officer and several to many technicians. The room buzzed like a disturbed beehive. Several dozen or more uniformed runners carrying Post-It notes, manilla folders and briefcases, some chained and locked to the runner's wrists, dashed from one temporary command center to another, as well as and in and out of various doors located strategically throughout the room. The subdued lighting and somber atmosphere offered the only hint of control. A small dias at the far end of the room surrounded by a half-circle bank of monitors being watched by frowning senior Cerebrus and military staff members, separated the raised platform from the rest of the room and at least made the chaos look purposeful.

What it all meant remained unclear, but the key to it all,

Stewart surmised, must lie in Laplacia where he immediately dispatched Falk. After ordering one of the agency's Gulfstreams at the nearest airport to be on alert for Falk, Koski, on Stewart's orders, settled in at Cerebrus headquarters to act as field liaison between Stewart and Falk. Her immediate job would be to make sense of everything that was going on and instantly relay that information to Falk.

Koski made no effort to hide her displeasure at being physically separated from Falk. They had become a highly skilled, two-person field team. Stewart, sensing Koski's barely hidden anger, tried unsuccessfully to explain the necessity, in his mind, of having her constantly informed and ready to travel elsewhere, should another event occur. His unquestionable logic, however, did little to diminish her feelings, the seemingly all encompassing chaos going on about her only heightening her concern.

Chapter 4

In Laplacia, Falk booked a room at the town's one and only motel, a run-down derelict from the 50's done in faux Hawaiian decor, then walked to its one and only cafe to grab some breakfast after his early morning flight arrival. In the cafe, he took a pedestal stool in the center of the long 'bar' and began chatting up the locals. Each of the men he politely interrogated proved, as expected, to be completely "small town" odd in character, manner, interests and voice. Each seemed wary, leading Falk to wonder whether, they might be culturally xenophobic. If so, good. That would mean they would be aware of anything at all out of the ordinary. The other possibility, of course, was that they were collectively hiding something. In the end, Falk ended up calling Koski and reporting that nothing at all related to the event appeared to have happened or be happening in the little town of two hundred.

Chapter 5

Stewart listened with one ear to Koski's near continuous grumbling at being separated from Falk, and with the other to her recount of Falk's uneventful phone report. Both jumped when a klaxon suddenly blared, a indication that an official cyber-attack alert had been issued.

Over the last few hours, reports of more and more small but potentially damaging computer "glitches" had begun streaming into Cerebrus' various command centers, as echo-ripples from the "non-event event" continued to spread out from Laplacia. Most worrisome, was a report that four American Air Force F-15E Strike Eagle interceptors passing through the widening, outermost echo-ripple's circumference simultaneously experienced a five-second loss of power before automatically re-powering.

A few minutes later, two Canadian CF-18 Hornets, flying wing-to-wing on a training mission out of Canadian Forces

Base at North Bay, Ontario, as they passed through the northern edge of the same echo-ripple, similarly lost power for several seconds and, momentarily helpless, crashed into each other, killing both airplanes' pilots and weapons systems officers.

Moments after that, a report came in from NSA that Internet browser giant UpOn reported ten seconds of simultaneous unexplained blackout in a thousand distributed servers located throughout a small town several miles southwest of where the F-15E Strike Eagles momentarily lost power, again just when the edge of the ripple passed over their location. The moment the wave passed, all the servers began rebooting at the same time, causing an electrical drain that triggered an area-wide electrical power network failure, further delaying return of the servers to normal operation.

Later, as the perimeter of the echo-ripple continued to spread outward, two trains on the Chicago to Washington DC route experienced a momentary loss of power, the one, twenty minutes ahead of the the other unable to restart, the one behind abruptly returning to power and colliding into the backend of its stalled sister, derailing both trains. Some of the passengers, including several congressmen, a high-ranking military officer and a high-profile industrialist, were reported dead. Injuries were being reported in the hundreds. It would have been the news story of the day had it been the only major catastrophe. Instead, it ended up an aside in that hour's television news report, lost in an ever-expanding number of accident reports from throughout the Northeast.

As the ripple expanded into Canada, Cerebrus began receiving reports of momentary computer shutdowns from domestic, government and Canadian military sites. One shutdown caused electronic stock prices in the Canadian Stock Exchange to flicker, and, in an attempt to auto-reboot and self-correct, display stock values at random lower or higher values. Ten minutes later, the values inexplicably returned to their pre-glitch prices but only after the error had triggered a full-scale "adjustment," initiated by millions of preprogrammed "buy" and "sell" orders. No one at this point had any idea how to actually correct the market, now in total chaos.

In Northeastern USA, city and state police were reporting a sudden rise in automobile accidents, most the result of momentary failures of electronic components within the cars. As a result, major TV news syndicates, at the request of Homeland Security, had begun advising people in the northeastern states not to drive unless it was an absolute emergency. The announcement caused further confusion as growing numbers of viewers and investigative journalists began calling in to ask if the sudden spates of accidents didn't themselves constitute an emergency.

The most serious automotive failures were those occurring in cars on multi-lane highways equidistant in any direction from Laplacia, as the echo-ripple's edge continued to expand outwards. A report came in of a two thousand car pile up on the first major interstate freeway encountering the ripple. Hundreds were being reported dead or injured on news flashes across the country. The ever-expanding "Circle of Death" as it was coming to be known, was not only causing cars and trucks to experience some seconds of complete loss of control—just enough to wreak havoc—but also causing those that were not permanently disabled to suddenly roar back to life to wreak further destruction and carnage.

The increasing numbers of auto accident reports were already causing the insurance industry and auto giants to begin seriously considering the financial and litigious consequences should the Circle of Death continue.

Chapter 6

Back in Laplacia, Falk was notified by Koski that the NSA cyber-geniuses now "mostly agreed" among themselves that the instigating event had indeed begun in Laplacia, as evidenced by the fact that the echo-ripples were continuing to spread out equally in every direction from there. Furthermore, the bizarre bidding for the Eastern American Seaboard had been, according to the latest reports by US cybersecurity and internet specialists, followed almost immediately by a massive exchange of electronic BitCoins. With BitCoins, the newest introduced form of world currency, the identity of sellers and buyers was electronically opaque even to NSA, fueling further concern of a coordinated cyber-attack of a manner and magnitude never before experienced.

The effect of the unprecedented exchange of BitCoins was now causing collateral damage of its own in participating American financial institutions, raising the specter of regional financial systems collapse. Anything that involved BitCoins, including online consumer purchases, gaming, bill payments, real estate transactions, even bank-to-bank currency exchanges, appeared endangered. The question on everyone's mind, including Stewart's, was what it all meant.

It was difficult to determine, NSA cybercrime technicians were assuring Cerebrus and thereby Koski and Falk, but still highly *likely,* that while the initial bids appeared to have come from a number of sources, a "final purchase" was completed between seller and buyer, the actual payment coming from a variety of different sources, located both within and outside the USA. The total purchase of the auction was currently estimated in excess of a trillion American dollars equivalent, an amount sufficient to instigate, inflate, deflate or even destroy the various world currencies depending on timing, collateral damage, and investor reactions. Homeland Security and the Department of the Treasury were questioning whether the unprecedented exchange of BitCoins represented an attempt to launder stashes of heretofore hidden "dark" money accumulated by international criminal organizations, possibly under the aegis of a newly organized cartel of criminal or terrorist organizations. Their questioning, unfortunately, remained speculative, in the end adding to the general confusion rather than mitigating it.

Two important pieces of information, however, had come to light, Koski informed Falk. First, the Circle of Death, as it continued to expand outward, was now slowly diminishing in strength, causing less damage to fewer digital electronic devices. Second, NSA and Cerebrus cyber-jockeys had confirmed that an unusual transmission had indeed been momentarily centered at a farmhouse registered to a Mister Aaron Hempsted, an elderly, retired man who lived alone on the outskirts of Laplacia.

Falk sighed, wished Koski well, signed off, and left the cafe to visit what he felt would likely prove to be one very dangerous old man.

Chapter 7

As Koski signed off, Stewart announced loudly in the background that a second event had occurred, again lasting only a fraction of a millisecond, and that, according to initial electronic failure reports, the epicenter this time was in Fulton, Ohio, another isolated country town with fewer than a couple hundred residents. Located due north of Columbus, it was a town like Laplacia that one had to work hard to locate on any map.

As with the first, the second event had initially passed undetected, its initial echo-ripples causing little damage other than a rash of irritating, momentary home computer failures at various nearby farms. Within several hours, however, Cerebrus situation room monitors were flashing reports of destruction and loss of life associated with the sudden collapse of the Central United States Power Interconnect and a regional power network in southern Canada. Interestingly, both networks had

had power nodes located where the echo-ripples from this new event converged with those from the first event. It quickly became clear that while damage from the first event echoes was diminishing, wherever those from the two events intersected, damage was vastly compounded.

Stewart was already beginning to wonder aloud if, even without corroborating evidence, the underlying purpose of the events was to produce specific event-echo intersections at key locations, and whether that reflected a highly sophisticated underlying strategic attack plan. If so, additional events would surely follow, and the number of intersections would increase exponentially, quickly overwhelming America's resources and ability to respond.

Even without proof, Stewart felt justified sending Koski to Fulton, while the various departments of the United States government, working together, continued to attempt to determine if the two incidents were actually connected, and, if so, if they were indeed harbingers of what Stewart suspected represented a massive cyberattack. No more stealing names, addresses, social security numbers, credit card numbers and government personnel files. If what he feared was true, this predicated all out cyber-warfare like the world had never before seen.

Chapter 8

Koski's drive to the airport left her feeling even more concerned and irritated at being apart from Falk. During their last assignment, code-named The Chemical Factor, each came frighteningly close to dying, and yet, in a surprise turn, each had snatched the other from certain death and the process had brought them closer together than ever before. Initially, she had had to focus all her efforts on being a superior agent for her unquestionably superior partner. Recently, however, occasional tugs of affection had begun popping out of nowhere, especially when they were in close physical proximity, more so when in danger. Falk had as much acknowledged the same. It seemed that danger was tempering their affection into something more akin to…what? Were they falling for each other? No! Neither could. Each carried too much past emotional baggage. Besides, they were professionals! Yet her awakening feelings were even now morphing from concern into an aching—or, was it a a longing—located deep in the center of her being.

Speeding along the freeway, musing over the new way she was coming to regard Falk, Koski missed the moment when her car engine suddenly died, and, shaken abruptly out of her reverie, panicked.

To her alarm, the engine, power steering and power brakes had all gone out. The only working device left was the manual hand brake, which she began pumping aggressively to slow the car and keep it from spinning out of control.

Koski had to marshal all her reserves to tease the fishtailing car to a stop. It was only when the car was resting silently on the shoulder of the freeway that she breathed a sigh of relief, then noticed the many other cars on the freeway knocking into each other like bumper cars, tearing at each other's plastic and metal exterior like angry dinosaurs fighting over their territories. As if that weren't enough, fifteen seconds later all undamaged car engines, including Koski's, abruptly roared back to life, hers lunging forward like a lioness springing for the kill, hitting the safety railing and bouncing the car back onto the active freeway.

Wrestling for control of the car while dodging vehicles flying at her from the left, right, ahead and behind, it was only a matter of time before one smashed smartly into the passenger side of her car and another immediately afterwards into the driver's side, causing her rental car's multiple airbags to deploy. No longer able to see, Koski fought both car and mounting claustrophobia, her stomach lurching, her initial panic quickly superseded by outright terror. Fighting the desperate feeling that she needed to exit what otherwise might become her tomb, but aware of the mortal danger of getting out with so many cars zooming and spinning out of control all about her, Koski plunged her hand under the gel-like folds of the now deflating front air bag until she could feel the ignition key in her fingers and turn off the engine. Drivers about her, seemingly on cue, began turning off their cars, or, reacquiring control, eventually braking them to a stop. The freeway soon looked like a spent battlefield, littered with damaged cars, smoking debris scattered everywhere, the continued brunt of the attack shooting like an arrow ahead up the freeway.

After checking carefully in every direction, Koski climbed out of her car and joined one of several lines of dazed drivers and passengers walking zombie-like in single file along the cluttered freeway.

Koski couldn't help but wonder if the sudden, eerie silence now closing about her, punctuated by the piercing cries of frightened children, was a premonition of something darker yet to come.

.

Chapter 9

Back in Washington DC, computer experts at Cerebrus headquarters huddled over one of the many super-computer displays to debate the validity and implications of a hastily prepared computer simulation of the effects of the so far two events. The terminal displayed the two event-location-points in pulsing red, each with ever-expanding, ever-intersecting, florescent-green, curved echo-ripple lines emanating outwards, overlaid on a hazy grey topological map of America. But the focus of the experts' concern wasn't so much on what the terminal was displaying, as it was on their speculation about the nature of the actual events, which seemed to appear out of nowhere and the next instant, disappear entirely. Unable to pursue their concern further, they turned their attentions to various interpretations of what appeared to be another auction. A huge monetary transaction had occurred fractions of a second after what looked like a frenetic burst of "bidding," ostensibly for possession of what they surmised to be the Eastern Central Region of the USA. As a result, the experts were falling into two groups: one focused on the events, the other on the auctions.

The first group continued discussing how it was that an event phenomenon of this magnitude could appear, then disappear without any indication at the source of having ever occurred. Initially branded a "freak anomaly," then "a non-real occurrence," the event recurrence had advanced it to being an actual, real, if momentary and incredibly puzzling, event.

"They seem to materialize from nowhere and instantly revert back to whatever they were before," a white-haired, sallow-faced physicist offered, awe apparent in every word.

"Fiddlesticks, Bert! Nothing can come from nothing!" a flame-red-haired, middle-aged mathematician, standing elbow-to-elbow with the physicist countered sharply as the two watched the resulting, now familiar echo rings continue to expand and intersect.

"But how, Francis? How? How do you explain...?" Bert asked.

"I can't! At least not yet," replied the mathematician. "But I'm certain an explanation will present itself. One more event and my group should have enough data to prove what we both know: The laws of physics require that nothing can come from nothing!"

"A couple of peculiar 'singular singularities', then? Some new kind of 'Little Big Bangs'?" offered Francis jokingly in challenge.

"A 'singular singularity'? What the heck does that mean, Bert? And while they may *look* like similar 'Little Big Bangs', mathematically, they can't be. The mathematics are all wrong. Their Circles of Death don't act like the result of *any* kind of bang or bump. The events are momentary, pin-point, time-space continuum disturbances. Like what would result from tossing a massively powerful but subatomic sized 'stone' into our particular time-space 'pond'. Or, given the presence of two events, maybe skipping a stone into it. I don't know, but in each case, I suspect a sudden, short-lived, though *very* powerful rent in time-space, though not in the electromagnetic sense as everything at the moment leads us to believe. Allowed to speculate, I'd say the two events are 'quantum explosions'. It's those damn enhancing waves where the ripples from each meet that make them…"

"More like quantum *im*plosions?" offered the first.

"Yes. Tiny quantum implosions! And incredibly powerful ones. As if an infinitesimal speck of space-time just suddenly vanished. Or collapsed. Then reappeared, or reorganized, or disappeared. I've asked my group to focus on looking, if you will, for a resulting 'fingerprint' that might tell us if what reappears after the event is exactly the same or slightly different from what disappeared at its beginning, and…"

The second group of specialists were busy speculating about the flow of BitCoins that had once again occurred, some saying just before, some just after, and others saying simultaneous with but not quite *completely* simultaneous with the events. Above the general din, it would sound to anyone listening from outside, that despite the awesome assemblage of experts, their respective agencies' massive, shared resources, and the group's best collective effort, no one yet really had a clue as to the source or destination of the BitCoins.

"It's like a damn Sujiko puzzle of the tenth or eleventh order…" began an economic analyst, shoving his hands in frustration into the back pockets of his frayed jeans, his branded heavy-metal-rocker t-shirt looking decidedly pre-adolescent despite the fuzzy stubble on his cheeks and chin.

"And you, Martin, how would you know a Sujiko from a Suduko puzzle?" teased a female colleague several years his younger, wearing an expensive, designer work jacket over a permanently-pressed white blouse and perfectly-matched black slacks and shoes.

"Eh?" the man replied, looking as if he actually didn't know the difference. "I mean, hey, it's all just another puzzle. A game.

A complex one, admittedly, but rationally solvable. All games are. Look, Jeebs: Assume n-sellers and m-buyers, each with an unknown amount of untraceable BitCoins, but each with a unique bid and purchase style. It's like someone's trying to hack their way with brute force into…"

"The key is the BitCoins, not the persons behind them," the young woman interjected with authority. "What we're seeing isn't anything like the n-dimensional construct you're proposing. As I see it, these are careful, cleverly constructed, business exchanges with a common, practical, underlying financial purpose. This isn't a puzzle, game or new kind of hack. It's a sophisticated crime, and everything resulting is part of a crime scene investigation. A mostly digital crime, perhaps, but a physical crime nonetheless. And, by the way, my name is Mary. Dr. Mary Johnson, not…"

"Oh, for Christ's sake, Jeebs! Take off your Sherlock Holmes' hat and leave that kind of mundane thinking behind. Climb into the rocket seat next to me and jet into the future, girl. Today's future! This isn't Hawaii-Five-O or NCSI.

Dr. Johnson looked floored.

"Everything said, Jeebs, I believe you're both right and wrong. You're right that, technically, it really *isn't* a new kind of puzzle, game or hack. I just said that to stimulate your intellectual hormones. In fact, there's no hacking involved at all. And the pre-event didn't *start* with anything digital or even internet-based, yet it's being *propagated* as if it were. In my mind, the event and the auction are, as you mentioned, clever, purposeful, and designed with a singular purpose in mind. But what we're facing is still a puzzle or game, a highly complex one with a hidden agenda, as I said before I was so rudely..." Jeans and T-Shirt replied.

In the end, neither agreed on anything except that, given the appearance of the second event and auction, something had *recurred* and, like the first auction, was associated with a major global financial exchange, the two taken together big enough to bring down countries.

Frowning, arms folded across his chest, Colonel Rellin stood resolute next to Stewart, the two a distance behind the mass of experts. Each encouraged his constituents to continue their work, Stewart, for the moment emphasizing the importance of developing testable hypotheses regarding the actual nature of the events, Rellin stressing documenting the flow of BitCoins. They concluded, reminding everyone of the importance of using any and all information to predict the location, timing, and expected results of a third such event and auction. In fact, no one was listening. Everyone was totally absorbed in solving his or her small part of the seemingly incomprehensible overall problem.

Stewart turned to Rellin and noticed the man's slumped shoulders. Walking out of the command center alongside each other and down the long hallway, they could each *feel* the other's exhaustion. As they went, Stewart overheard some Cerebrus aides huddled together in front of a closed door, discussing the absurdity of "buying" regions of the USA, and decided, like them, that the whole "sale of property" scenario was simply too outrageous. Like Jeans-And-T-Shirt had said, there had to be more to it than the auctioning off of the United States of America. There had to be an *endgame*, and it was his job to uncover it. For the moment, he might not be able to explain the who, what, when, where or even how, but knowing the why was what his work was all about, and knowing it was what typically gave Cerebrus the edge it needed to successfully resolve even the most opaque threats. His strength had always been to play to the "why," and with that solidly in mind, he rethought recent events.

The best "why" he could figure right now, was that the *events* had been carefully located so that their "echoes" would intersect at specific locations that would invoke maximum disruption. There had to be a greater purpose to the events than what was so far visible. The part that kept nagging at him was whether they were a prelude to a larger plan to bring the USA to its knees. But if so, why only brief failures? Why temporary disruption rather than permanent destruction? The only explanation he could come up with was that someone wanted to paralyze, but not permanently damage the nation.

As for the *auctions*, this *had* to be a diversion—a huge red herring—designed to engage and deflect America's intelligence resources away from the less well defined events.

That took him full circle back to the events: There *had* to be something more behind them than the temporary power disruptions. Perhaps they were meant to humiliate the United States? To scare its citizenry into frenetic mis-action? Or perhaps these first two events were merely tests of something more sinister, like Hitler testing his newest weapons of war on unsuspecting populations during the Spanish Civil War.

Stewart's best plan was to continue personally directing Cerebrus' two finest resources, Koski and Falk, to scour the two event locations for any clues as to what might actually be going on. He needed more information in order to proceed with identifying the *why*. The rest would follow: *who* might be causing the events, *when* more events might occur, and exactly *how* "they," whoever they were, were causing the events to happen, as currently held, "out of the blue." Frustrated, heels clicking on the polished tiles, he broadcast a challenging scowl to anyone unlucky enough to glance at him—which, given the situation, meant no one.

Stewart squared his shoulders. For now, he needed to trust in the abilities of his two finest, and wait for something useful from them, or for a third event to occur. Either way, he needed a greater pattern to emerge.

Chapter 10

In Laplacia, Falk rolled his rental car to a stop in front of the Hempsted residence. Sliding his legs out, he stopped on impulse and reached inside the glove compartment. Removing his automatic, he placed it in his well-worn shoulder holster.

Standing before the dilapidated old house with it's cracked, boarded, dirt-opaque windows, he removed the gun, released the safety, chambered a round, and held the weapon at ready behind his thigh.

The moment he rapped on the door, it cracked open, and through the slit a single eye fixed warily on him. Falk took a step back, searching unsuccessfully for the rest of the answerer's face. What little he could see fit how the townsfolk had described Aaron Hempsted: A rheumy eye floated in a drawn, bloodless vertical slit of elongated face, topped by a wisp of uncombed white hair. The crack opened slightly more to reveal a pair of thin, tightly closed lips above a stubbly chin.

"Wha'd'ya want?" growled the lips, barely moving.

"Mr. Hempstead? Mr. Aaron Hempsted?" Falk asked, his sixth sense warning him not to relax for even a second.

As the two talked, Hempsted slowly cracked the door further, enough for Falk to make out the man's shoddy, disheveled clothes.

Falk's grip on his weapon tightened.

Over the next few minutes, Hempsted carefully avoided answering every one of Falk's questions, essentially giving out no information beyond his name. During their talk, the door opened slightly wider and clunked against a fully extended door chain.

It didn't take long for Falk to discern that Hempsted was elderly and unclear in thought, which would make the man, at best, computer-challenged. Concluding the old man couldn't possibly be behind the event, Falk inquired if anyone else lived in the dusty-smelling, unkempt house he could see above the hunched man's white-haired head.

Hempsted paused, then hesitantly related that he was renting an upstairs room to two girls in their late teens. When Falk asked their names, the old man's white eyebrows crinkled, merging in the center of his forehead, and he became obstinately defensive, saying only that they weren't home.

When Falk asked if it would be possible to see their room,

Hempsted become agitated and ordered him coarsely off the porch and property.

Odd way for a person to act, even a recluse, thought Falk on his way back to the car. As he climbed in, he noticed out of the corner of his eye a flash of light off an odd-looking, rooftop satellite dish, its antenna wire winding its way into the upstairs bedroom window.

Chapter 11

At the airport, Koski negotiated the next available flight to Columbus, reflecting uneasily on the anxiety that being cooped up in a confined space like a small commuter aircraft always caused her. It was a "gift" from her traumatic childhood.

These days, the resulting anxiety attacks had a habit of occurring out of the blue, much like the present "events," ending just as abruptly as they began, leaving her with an uncomfortable, stunned feeling. The most distressing thing about them, however, was knowing that they would return again and again, typically when she least expected it, until she exited the tight enclosure that had brought them on.

Barely twenty minutes into the flight, acutely missing Falk's reassuring presence, her nerves frayed, she fell into an exhausted sleep.

Moments later, the mesmerizing hiss of the air conditioners and whine of the engines abruptly cut out.

For a while the plane continued knifing silently forward through the air. Sensing her body floating above the seat, she felt rather than saw the planes nose begin to decline ever-so-slowly until the aircraft entered a steep dive. A series of pops, and a rain of oxygen masks deployed. Mothers, too stunned to reach for a mask, clutched their children. Some whimpered with fear. Others screamed. It was at precisely that moment the full-fledged anxiety attack she'd been awaiting gripped her.

The plane, nose down forty-five degrees, continued to fall soundlessly through the air through one after another thick layer of clouds for perhaps ten thousand stomach-wrenching feet by Koski's panicked mind's auto-calculation before the cabin lights and engines suddenly came back on.

The plane shuddered.

Outside, a metallic scream arose as the wings and fuselage tried to respond to the air crew's frantic attempt to halt the plane's descent. Kiosk's body weight abruptly quadrupled and passengers throughout the plane began taking up the children's screams.

The next ten seconds seemed like an hour. The plane was now at so low an altitude she could make out through her window the different colored clothes people in a large parking lot below were wearing, and see the whites of their eyes, wide in horror, staring up at the falling airplane.

Hands shaking, she tried to call Falk only to drop the phone, and upon retrieving it, find that it was irreparably damaged.

Bracing for what could only be a fatal impact, Koski jerked awake when the flight attendant tapped her shoulder saying, "Fasten your seat belt, please. We're coming into Columbus." Clutching her seat arm rests in a vise-like grip, her knuckles white and bloodless, she looking frantically out her window to see that the plane was, indeed, gently descending for landing.

Her confidence thoroughly shaken, she couldn't help but wonder if the 'daymare' she had just experienced was yet another premonition of what was to come.

Chapter 12

In Columbus, Koski rented a car only to have to fight her way to Fulton on packed roads. It reminded her of a mission with Falk in which they'd become entangled in a similar traffic snarl. In her mind she could hear Falk's voice saying he felt like a spawning salmon trying to fight its way upstream. Koski couldn't help but grin at the thought. The ethereal sound of his voice lingering in her head helped calm her.

Just before her exit, the rental car shuddered, stopped running, and plowed, *sans* brakes and steering, off the highway, slowing to a near stop as it rolled onto the shoulder. As it approached the safety railing, it abruptly roared back to life, slamming through the railing and surging on towards a massive Fulton city signpost.

Koski wrestled the rental car to a stop inches from the signpost. Her GPS locator on the passenger seat was on the floor in pieces. Noting a Fulton police SUV parked behind the signpost, she got out, flashed her federal agent identification and requested assistance in locating the geographic epicenter of the second event using their police GPS and the coordinates Stewart had provided.

Though wary, the male officer and his more sympathetic female compatriot put away their radar gun and entered the coordinates into their GPS locator, determining it to be those of "Old Man Thorsdan's farm" located on the outskirts of the city. At their invitation, Koski parked her rental car and jumped in the police SUV. The next thing she knew, she and the two officers were cruising down a side road. The policewoman pointed out the window at an infinite line of heavily weathered fenceposts whipping by the passenger side of the SUV, explaining that they marked the border of what used to be a large commercial ranch and farm. The greying wood fenceposts contrasted sharply in the late, almost florescent afternoon sun against a distant, growing darkness.

By the time they arrived at the entrance gate, turned right and continued down a bumpy, weed-overgrown dirt roadway, dusk had fallen, requiring the driver to turn on the vehicle's headlamps. Between their present location and the farmhouse was a single, intervening hill.

Proceeding, the policeman pulled the SUV to a stop atop the rise. In the distance, at the end of the straight-line dirt road, the three could just make out a lightless, matchbox-sized house and barn located atop a lightly wooded hill.

Resuming their approach, the house and barn resolved into a more weathered, dark and abandoned couple of dwellings than Koski had at first imagined. Black clouds, pregnant with rain, were gathering immediately above the two buildings, creating a suffocating blanket of silence about the car so profound that Koski could hear the breathing of the driver and the heartbeat of his assistant.

Koski unrolled her window to get a better look. The air outside had had become so heavy that when she stuck out her hand, tiny raindrops began forming, tracing a path through the otherwise still air.

After rattling over an old livestock grating, the SUV began climbing the final hill. As they went, Koski could make out numerous large pens, each devoid of animals. At the top of the hill, between what looked like an abandoned house and barn was an old, gray-primer-coated Ford truck with several bundles of hay piled in its bed. As they approached the farm house, the hairs on the back of Koski's neck reflexively stood.

The SUV pulled to a stop and Koski started to climb out, then, on impulse, removed her automatic from its shoulder holster. The two police officers remained in the SUV, staring at the black, foreboding house and the armed agent slipping and sliding her way through the wet mud and up the wooden porch steps.

At the top of the steps, Koski paused, hand in mid-air, about to knock on the rickety screen door, when she sensed movement inside and, having second thoughts, released the safety, chambered a round, and held the readied weapon down at her side. Flattening her back against the wall, she rapped loudly on the edge of the screen door. The weather-warped door clacked noisily with each strike.

A few moments later, an old man cracked open the inside door, and eyed Koski warily. "Wha' d'ya want?"

"Good evening, Mister…" Koski began.

"Thorsdan. Name's Thorsdan. An' why in God's name would the likes of you be a-comin' to a place like this, in this kind a weather and at such an hour?" he asked breathlessly.

"Mr. Thorsdan," Koski began again. "I've been asked to come here to investigate…"

"Nothin' here t'vestigate, young lady. Nothin' a'tall. I suggest you mind yur business an' leave." After the briefest pause, he re-summarized: "In case you didn't catch what I jus' said, it means 'git the hell off my land'. Now!"

The female officer in the SUV watched Koski and Old Man Thorsdan talk. After a few minutes, she nudged her partner with an elbow and reached unobtrusively for her weapon.

Koski attempted to continue engaging the crotchety old man, but try as she might, she couldn't. Furthermore, she couldn't imagine him being any part of the highly sophisticated technological "event" the two police had assured her had definitely originated on his farm. Recalling the truck, she inquired politely if there were any farmhands present.

The old man half-mumbled, half-complained about "a couple a' no-good rascal girls" who had contacted him during a trip into town to pick up supplies.

"They tol' me they waz farm hands, tho' I doubted 'em right away from th' look of their pristine hands." Nonetheless, he'd signed them on about a month ago, he said. They'd agreed to help him fix up the house and barn in return for free room and board. The problem was, the old man continued, typical of young folks today, they didn't ever get around to doing any fixing. Instead, they spent most of their time "holed up in the barn, playin' video games."

When Koski asked if she could meet them, the gruff old man became agitated, and told her he'd "said enough for one night," repeating his demand that she leave. Now.

On her way back to the SUV, a slapping noise directed her attention to the barn where a wire from a new-looking satellite dish on the roof was flapping in the wind and repeatedly striking the side of the barn. The cable disappeared through a crack in the first floor siding.

It wasn't so much the presence of the satellite dish or the cable that bothered her as it was that the line was directed into the least likely place she could imagine. Not the farmhouse, but the old, dilapidated animal barn where the two girls, according to Thorsdan, liked to "hole up." Strange.

Chapter 13

Back in the Cerebrus Situation Room in Washington DC, a gaggle of computer technicians were noisily discussing the displayed echo-waves on the big board emanating outwards from the first and second point-sources for the umpteenth time. While each set of echo-waves was clearly diminishing in strength as it spread, particular mayhem occurred everywhere echo-waves from the two Circles of Death intersected. Furthermore, whenever an intersection occurred immediately outside a high-rise urban center, some of the waves deflected off the larger buildings, effectively creating a new point-source and, from it, a spate of new waves emanated, creating a new Circle of Death and a spate of new intersections with their attendant electrical shutdowns.

It was clear now that it was the intersections that were causing the greatest damage to everything electrical or electronic. All available computational resources were being called upon to help predict the exponentially increasing number of point-sources and intersections in order to provide citizens a few minutes warning before the havoc. Reports continued coming in from regional, even national—most often military—centers of command and control located throughout the Americas, and none were encouraging. After recovering from a temporary shutdown, security at one after another installation was switching to high, meaning deadly force, alert.

How many more of these events, each propagating yet more echo-waves, back-echoes, point-sources and intersections can we survive? Stewart pondered. *What good is 'purchasing' a crippled region for billions, even trillions of dollars when it's damaged and not legally possessable?*

His thoughts were interrupted by a call from Koski that had been patched into the local DC police network and forwarded to him. The two were immediately joined in conference call by Falk on his cellular. Both agents conveyed their sites as lacking anything unusual on inspection, other than the presence at both sites of a single, elderly person (not really all that unusual), renting out a room to two youths (an interesting congruity), both sites having new TV satellite antennas (probably not all that unusual for an isolated country locale). As for the barn cable that concerned Koski, perhaps, as the two local police officers had jokingly suggested, Thorsdan was a progressive farmer, providing entertainment for his animals.

Is it possible, Stewart found himself considering while he listened, *that the computed event epicenters might not be the actual source epicenters?*

Ridiculous, he chided mentally, while grabbing the first passing computer geek for a quick hallway consult regarding the idea. The geek listened, only to shake his head dismissively at having been subjected to so incredibly stupid an idea before moving on.

Stewart conveyed the result of his hallway consultation to Falk and Koski.

For Falk, the emerging question was *how* the events were actually being brought about; for Koski, it was whether the abruptness of each of the farmer's requests for her and Falk to leave *might indicate something much bigger and darker.*

"Add cleverer and inherently evil," added Falk, "and I'll have to agree."

While Stewart quickly reassessed his agents' observations, hypotheses and suggestions, a voice on the building's public address system interrupted, announcing that a third event had just occurred, this time in Red River, Montana. Voice activity in the command center where Stewart was standing abruptly ceased, then resumed at a rapidly increasing level until it drowned out any hope of further conversation with his two field agents. Stewart yelled into his phone for Koski and Falk to stay where they were, and continue nosing about their respective epicenters, deciding in that moment to return, albeit briefly, from management to field work, to look into the newest event himself.

Chapter 14

At the Laplacia Diner, Falk returned his cell phone to his pocket and his attention to his now stone-cold plate dinner and to *how* exactly the now *three* events might have been created. A single event could have been the result of some kind of unusual 'natural' event. Two events could still be a 'natural' coincidence, though it would be unlikely. But three, regularly spaced events, all causing similar effects, suggested decidedly human intervention.

How are these events being created? Falk mulled.

Individually, the events seemed to him to most resemble an electromagnetic pulse, or EMP. EMP's, however, were typically associated with a nuclear blast. Given his and Koski's sites were physically intact, an EMP clearly couldn't have started there. It was, of course, possible that these were some new kind of EMP. On the other hand, non-nuclear EMPs, or NNEMP's, were still on the drawing board, and, even so, weren't predicted to result in waves that, upon intersecting, *multiplied* in strength.

A sudden electrostatic discharge or ESD, much like a lightning strike, could interrupt and damage nearby electronic devices, but, again, hadn't ever been known to cause echo-ripples or new reflective point-sources to occur. In addition, an ESD would directly effect living things as well.

No, the events could be *likened* to EMPs or ESDs, and they probably were being so likened in civilian and military centers throughout North America. But in deference to his partner, Koski, he had to admit, these events had the feel of something more. Something, as she said, dark, sinister and directed. As if behind everything lurked a malevolent intelligence—clever and ruthless—testing and flexing its muscles.

So far, his and Koski's sites had yielded few relevant clues as to the *how* of the events, other than the implication that they were, indeed, unique in nature. Something never before experienced. As he sat, he reviewed yet again everything that was currently known about the first two events:

In each case, the initializing event occurred suddenly and unexpectedly.

In each case, the event seemed centered in an isolated backcountry location.

In each case, an old man was housing two "difficult" youngsters. *That was interesting.*

In each case, there was no sign on cursory examination of any technology other than a TV satellite dish.

Finishing his cold dinner and washing it down with an equally cold, viscous cuppa, Falk decided to focus on the satellite dish. It could be nothing more than an improved, television antenna made specifically for use in the backcountry, but it could also be a specially designed satellite up- or down-link. If so, it would likely be attached to an equally specialized receiving device.

Trying without success to recall in exactly which direction the satellite dish had been pointed, he grabbed his cold-weather coat, pulled a twenty out of his wallet and tucked it under the saucer of the empty coffee cup. Returning to his car, he commiserated that, despite the hour, he needed to determine in exactly which direction the antenna was pointed and somehow get a look inside the room the cable entered.

Chapter 15

At the Regent Hotel Cafe in Fulton, Ohio, Koski, like Falk, ended her call. While reiterating her experience at the Thorsdan farmhouse to Stewart and Falk, the feeling of evilness again prickled her spine. To Koski, it was more than just a hunch. The old man was off-putting, but, on careful reconsideration, he seemed not as much off-putting as…scared. Yes, that was it. Fearful. There had to be a connection of some kind between the event, the isolated farmhouse, the reticent owner, and the two boarders she had yet to meet and interview, and, with deference to her partner, the satellite dish with its wire going, at her site, into an animal barn of all places.

Koski raised her hand to call for the bill for her late night dinner.

Her waiter responded immediately. The young, lanky, sallow-complexioned boy of perhaps seventeen stopped in front of her table, shifted his weight onto one leg, and rested a hand jauntily on his lower hip. "You're new to Fulton," he stated, his inquisitiveness enhanced by his deep, post-adolescent voice. "Haven't seen you hereabouts before."

Koski nodded in the affirmative. "I dropped in to Fulton to visit…a relative. 'Old Man Thorsdan' people call him around here. He lives on a large farm-ranch on the outskirts of town. He's getting old and I heard he had had to hire a couple of young girls to…"

"Yeah. Know him. He's my sort of honorary uncle. Doesn't much come to town, and when he does, everyone mostly avoids him. It's like even though he's there, he's never really there, if you know what I mean. Those two girls on the other hand, when they come to town, they stick out like a sore thumb. Strange. Uncle Thorsdan never mentioned you."

"What do you mean by 'stick out…?'" Koski began her inquiry, only to be interrupted a second time in mid-sentence.

"I mean that, like you, they aren't from these parts. Oh, they're both pretty enough. One's a classic Oriental beauty. She never talks to anyone but her fairy-partner, and then they talk in some language that's definitely not English. Foreign. Sounds Japanese or Chinese."

Feeling irritated at being repeatedly interrupted, Koski tried again. "Can you describe…"

"Sorry. Can't. Well, won't, really," he said, removing his

hand from his hip. Placing both elbows on the table and leaning forward, he whispered conspiratorially, "I *like* my job here, see, and that means 'no gossiping'. I just thought…well, you being alone, and…"

It was Koski's turn to interrupt. The young man's attempt at a pickup was lame. It sounded as if he'd taken it from of an old 1940's movie. "I'm not 'alone', and while I appreciate your concern, I'm more interested in what you can tell me about your 'uncle's' boarders. Especially the Oriental. What…'"

"It's like I said, " he interrupted a fourth time. Looking over his shoulder to the left, then right, and, satisfied no one was watching or listening, he sat down beside her. "I don't want to start any rumors, see, but there was something definitely… *weird*…about them. Both of them. They were like, more than friends, but clearly not sisters or family, if you take my meaning. That reminds me, how exactly are you related?" The waiter paused, clearly expecting an answer.

"What did the Oriental look like?" Koski asked, carefully directing the conversation away from her factitious relationship to his "honorary" uncle back to her interest at hand. "Describe her. How tall is she? How old is she? How much do you think she weighs? Is she tall and thin? Short and stocky? What color are her hair and eyes?"

"Well, like I said, they don't much come to town, and, to be honest, I only really saw them once. Don't know much about the height and weight of the pretty Oriental, but she was shorter than her partner. Maybe a little older, too. I think her hair was black. Yeah. Come to think of it, it was jet black. And combed straight. Don't recall the color of her eyes, but they were suspicious looking. Like those Oriental spies you see in the movies. You know, 'spy-eyes'. Not at all like yours…"

"Yes, well, how about her partner? Can you describe her?" Koski introjected, trying again to keep the focus of the discussion on the two girls.

"Hmm. Well, she wasn't as interesting as the other. Taller. Thinner. Younger. Kinda clingy. She kept watching her partner, as if she needed permission to talk. To me, they looked and sounded like mismatched lovers. But why so much interest in these two? Name's Josh, by the way. People hereabouts say I'm pretty handsome and much more interesting…" Josh extended a hand and, without asking, latched onto Koski's, covering their momentarily joined hands with his other. After nervously looking about, he released her hand, leaving a small piece of paper in it. When Koski looked startled, Josh nodded, ahem'ed and said simply, "Your bill," then stood and walked away.

Examining the actual bill that Josh had earlier placed on the table, Koski reached in her wallet for a fifty and slipped it under the foot of her empty wine glass, clutching the piece of paper her waiter had palmed into her other hand after their brief and marginally helpful conversation.

Outside the restaurant and back in her car, she turned on the overhead car light and opened her hand to examine the tightly-folded piece of paper. When unfolded to eight times it's former size, it boasted a handwritten telephone number and two words: "Call me."

Chapter 16

Stewart was driven to a small private airport to board one of Ceberus' private charter jets. Mister Rellin had called ahead to Cerebrus' chief mechanic, Max, a lanky ex-marine combat officer and aircraft engineer who, once inside an engine space, seemed to sprout two additional hands. Max had jerry-rigged Farraday cages around the engine's computer, radar, GPS and radio to hopefully avert any loss of electricity should the plane pass through an event-wave or an intersection not predicted by computer models. Whether they would work or not was anyone's guess. In fact, predictions about the paths of waves and moment-to-moment number of intersections were growing super-exponentially, and were already taxing the capacity of the Cerebrus' most advanced computational resources.

Stewart's flight to the airport nearest Red River, Montana, was uneventful. Upon arriving in Red River proper, Stewart had barely settled in at the only local motel, when an intersection hit, plunging his room into total darkness. Power, surprisingly, was restored in less than ten seconds. Apparently people in Red River, including the motel, had emergency power generators. And emergency food, emergency water, emergency clothing, as well as emergency guns and ammunition. The parking lot outside the motel restaurant was apparently the *de facto* emergency meeting place, and it suddenly bristled with what looked like a rapidly forming military commando squad composed of rough-hewn survivalists, gathered about several four-wheel drive "monster" trucks.

"What the hell's going on?" asked a man wearing camouflaged body armor, cradling a fully automatic assault rifle in his arms. Stewart watched the man nervously flick the safety on and off, as if suffering from a neurological tick.

"Someone's jerked our power supply. Radios, cell phones, appliances, cars, hell, even our ham radio operators all went temporarily dead."

"Most are up and running again," offered another "commando," apparently their default commander.

"Damn Ruskies!" called out a woman, all in black, brandishing a modified AK-47 in the air. A black head scarf hid her face, revealing only two, red, and to Stewart's trained power of observation, scared eyes. "God-damn..."

"It ain't the Ruskies, Helen," returned the commander, speaking as much to her as to the other twenty or so armed men and women in varying degrees of combat dress. "More likely the Chinese. 'Been waiting for 'em to make a move on the good ol' USA for several decades. If it is them, they're in for one hell-uv-a-surprise if they get this far!"

The crowd shouted back a single loud "Huzzah!" in perfect commando unison.

"An' who the hell are you?" asked the commander, noting Stewart on the sidelines holding a government-issue pistol at his side, looking like a bewildered child who'd stumbled into a covert military field operation.

"Stewart," he replied curtly. "I'm from Washington." Stewart flashed his wallet identification, then snapped the wallet shut and replaced it in his hip pocket. "I'm here to investigate a power pulse that is said to have originated some time ago in the Red River area. There's no need for weapons…"

"Right," said the commander, smiling laconically while he and the rest of the Red River's self-made soldiers stared at Stewart's gun. "Right…"

"Right," echoed Stewart, replacing the weapon into it's shoulder holster and very slowly pulling out a map, hoping by the action to de-escalate the situation.

The crowd murmured, then began approaching in an ever-closing circle.

Stewart made a show of laying out the government topographic map on the hood of the nearest huge, black, jacked-up, off-road mega-truck. The ninja woman pulled out a military-issue flashlight and shined its beam on the map. "Right here, in fact," he continued, pointing at a spot some distance from where they were gathered.

"That's the Jersey place," a voice volunteered anonymously from within the crowd.

"The Jerseys," the commander repeated, his deprecatory tone revealing that they were not valued members of the elite force surrounding Stewart. "Old Man Jersey and his wife. Their homestead's located right beneath your finger. Those two might as well not exist at all, as they refuse to be part of our militia 'ready force'. Hardly see 'em in town anymore since they took on boarders. One of 'em's a foreigner."

Stewart looked up at a chorus of bobbing heads and yeah's. "What kind of foreigner?" asked Stewart, his interest piqued.

"Oriental. 'The Boss' we call her. Chinese, Japanese, Korean, hell, all 'em Orientals look the same. In this town, we don't like foreigners, period."

"How about the other?" inquired Stewart.

"Nice country girl. American, though not from here. Maybe

from Nebraska. She seems to look up to The Boss. Ought to be the other way around, if you ask me," the commander offered. Once again heads bobbed, followed by a chorus of yeah's.

"Could you take me there?" asked Stewart, unsure whether to broach either event or auction details with these people. Stewart's request proved a balm to the mob's frayed nerves. Trigger fingers relaxed. Everyone suddenly seemed interested in helping the "government man."

"Sure," acknowledged their commander. "Frey! Smart! Lexington! Come with me," he barked, signaling them with his hand. "The rest of you go into the restaurant and wait. We'll take my 'horse'," he continued, indicating with his thumb the monster crew-cab truck on the hood of which Stewart's map was positioned.

Quietly refolding the map and replacing it in the inside pocket of his coat, Stewart climbed up into the cab and assumed the passenger seat. Peering behind him, he watched two men slide into the back seat followed by the jihadist-looking woman swathed in black. Each sat stiffly, weapon at ready on his or her lap.

"Name's Greyside," the commander said, offering a large ham of a left hand, it's back covered with wiry black hair, while inserting the truck key into the ignition slot with his right. The behemoth's instant awakening growl, followed by several diesel knocks and another louder growl reminded Stewart of an Abrams tank engine being cold-started. "I'm the leader of the Red River Militiamen…" he chatted, adding quickly after glancing in his rearview mirror, "…and Militia women, of course."

On the way to the farm, Stewart attempted to question the group about the Jerseys but to no avail. To the group, the Jerseys were little more than ignorant homesteaders, and the two girls unwanted foreigners.

Chapter 17

Falk inched his rental car quietly up the driveway of the Hempsted residence. The dilapidated old house with it's boarded up windows somehow looked colder and even more uninviting than before. At first he couldn't put his finger on it, but walking up the rickety steps, it hit him: The front door that Aaron Hempsted had reluctantly cracked open and kept chain-locked throughout their talk on the last visit was now ajar, the door's rusted hinges squeaking ominously with each change in the night breeze. Shoulder against the side of the building to provide the least possible target, Falk called out several times without receiving any response. Carefully removing his automatic from his shoulder holster and slipping off the safety, he grasped the door's edge and called directly inside. Again, no answer except for another hinge squeak, this time caused by Falk's further opening the door.

After his eyes adjusted to the darkness, he noticed a shock

of white hair above the back of an easy chair facing away from him.

"Mr. Hempsted. It's Agent Falk," he said working his way through the door and cautiously around to the front of the chair. "I visited you earlier, and was wondering if we might…"

Aaron Hempsted was sitting, head erect, rheumy bloodshot eyes staring fixedly at Falk, his mouth limply agape, his unshaven face even whiter than before. A bloodless hand gripped each of the threadbare chair arms, making it appear as if he were pushing himself back into the seat. A small rivulet of dark, coagulated blood had worked its way alongside his nose and down one cheek from a small, round entry hole in the middle of his forehead. The man's shocked expression was accentuated by a halo of red splattered behind the man's resting head onto a white embroidered doily draped over the back of the easy chair.

Falk squatted, raised his weapon and held it with both hands as he swept the room. Recalling the old man saying that he was renting an upstairs room to two girls, he located a curved stairway and worked his way silently up. As he reached the top, he was startled by a girl's scream followed by a the report of a small-caliber pistol. Crouching on the floor and surveying the dark hallway for where they might have come, he was about to press forward when another report sounded, this time coming without a doubt from behind the first closed door on his left.

Reacting with the trained agility of a professional agent, he sprang forward and assumed a low position, his back flat against the side of the wooden door jamb, gun braced at the ready. As he shifted his weight to smash his way in, the door abruptly flew open. A short body in a billowy chiffon dress exited backwards, bumped into him and bounced back into the room falling on the floor with a loud clump. A cloud of whitish-grey smoke hung shoulder height about the room. The smoke had the familiar, acrid smell of gunpowder.

Sprinting though the now open door and into the room, Falk noticed directly in front of him a young Caucasian girl lying limp on her back in a rapidly enlarging pool of blood, her eyes staring fixedly upward, her forehead pierced with the same telltale hole he'd seen moments ago on Aaron Hempsted's forehead. To his right a slightly older Asian girl was scrambling for a small handgun on the floor. Falk raised his gun and shouted, but the girl was so agile she recovered the weapon before he finished, turned it in her hands to point, not at him but at herself, and pulled the trigger. The girl's body shuddered, then slammed against the right wall, the weapon, a Chinese-made Type 77, dropping to the ground in front of her lifeless body.

Chapter 18

In her car outside the Regent Hotel Cafe in Fulton, Ohio, Koski considered calling the handwritten telephone number she'd been palmed by her nervous waiter, Josh.

The young man was assumedly privy to some information, or, at least, he'd made it sound as if he were, but (and "but" was the operative word here), she had a bad feeling about him. "Call me," the note said, followed by a local phone number. That was all. Reading the words again, it felt to her like an invitation to danger. The lingering sense of danger, and her need to know more about Thorsdan paired with the earlier feeling of frank evilness while at the farm, all shouted caution. Both Josh and the old man had appeared…scared. In her mind she didn't doubt there was a link between the event, the dark farmhouse, the reticent owner, the two boarders, the odd-looking satellite dish, and, call it as she now saw it, Josh's fear.

Nervously fingering her cell phone, Koski reviewed in her

mind what she'd learned thus far from Josh: There were two "weird" girls. The first was a black-haired Asian, shorter and older than the second, who was less well described, other than being taller, thinner and "clingy." Maybe frightened. What was it he'd said exactly? "She kept watching the other, as if she needed her permission to talk?" Something like that. The second girl was, then, likely being controlled and could very well be nearly frightened to death. That made both of them especially dangerous.

Koski placed her cell phone on the passenger seat beside her. It would be awhile before Josh finished his shift, and Koski was feeling pressured to find out something—anything —about this second event. Exchanging the cell phone for her rental car keys, she tucked away the phone and inserted the master key into the car's ignition slot. Cautiously turning it recalled the recalcitrant but responsive car to life.

The drive to the Thorsdan farm proved even creepier than her first visit.The long line of weathered fenceposts reminded her of the owner's edginess which had morphed into a definite warning when she'd asked about his boarders.

After clawing up the muddied dirt road to the old farmhouse, the car rattled loudly over the livestock grating, and, as it did, Koski once again experienced that sense of profound silence that had so unnerved her the first time. The animal pens were still empty. The Ford truck she'd noted before, however, was gone.

As she prepared to climb out, she removed her automatic from its shoulder holster, holding it to her side and behind so as not to seem threatening. The farmhouse looked exactly like it did before but darker and more deserted, if that was possible.

Walking sideways up the creaky, wooden porch steps, Koski paused, recalling Old Man Thorsdan's brusque, intimidating manner. Stepping up to the door, she rapped on the screen door. There was no answer, but across the yard, she caught a movement inside the barn out of the corner of an eye.

That might be one of the two female "farm hands" Thorsdan had taken in to help restore the farm in return for free room and board. She wanted to meet and question both, but even more, she wanted to continue her interrogation of the old man. Anything she could get him to reveal would prove helpful when confronting the two girls.

Returning her gaze to the old house against which her shoulder was resting, she did a quick resurvey of the outside, the animal pens, then the barn, noting as before that none showed the slightest sign of restoration. In fact, the farm as a whole looked like it was about to fall apart. Peeking through an open crack in a broken, dirty window, it looked to her like no one was home.

It was then the movement that had caught her eye before repeated itself, this time directing her attention to a long black cable from the roof antenna, thudding loudly against the side of the barn. The wire snaked down the barn and disappeared into a crack in the siding where Koski assumed the two boarders kept the video game equipment about which Old Man Thorsdan had so vociferously complained.

Noting that, she returned her attention to where the old pickup truck had been parked. The bales of hay that had been in its bed were sitting haphazardly to the right and left of a set of bald tire marks which stretched on down to the approach road. Whoever drove the truck must have left very recently, she thought, given the clarity of the tire impressions, either carrying something else in its bed or having emptied it in anticipation of picking up something. Given the state of the house, she assumed the driver was Thorsdan. If indeed the old man had left, there would be no further advantage in waiting to talk with the girls.

The wind picked up, ruffling her hair and cracking the cable smartly against the side of the distant barn.

Abandoning the house, Koski crept cautiously to the front of the barn, where she located a chin-high open window and peered in, searching for where the cable entered.

It was difficult to make out anything in the darkness except the slightly blacker silhouettes of a large table with what looked like a pile of boxes on it. A moment later, her eyes adjusted enough for her to see that the boxes covered only half of the table and were, in fact, individual electronic devices dotted with scales, knobs and switches. *An odd collection and arrangement of video game boxes*, she thought. None appeared to be turned on. Scanning the room, she saw no signs of movement, so she slipped in.

What she saw as she cautiously approached the table piqued her immediate interest: The labels on the electronic devices were mostly handwritten in what looked like Chinese characters. What she saw next sent chills down her spine: Each "box" had two bullet holes in it. Walking closer, she tripped over something that chilled her even more: a wooden chair lying on its back in the dirt cradling the limp body of a young girl. The girl's face was turned to the side, but there was little question about her state. She, like each of the electronic boxes, had been the recipient of two slugs. Koski checked for a neck pulse, and feeling none, did a cursory survey of the body, realizing in the process she was standing in a pool of bloody mud.

Her senses heightened and her mind now on high alert, Koski crouched low and swept the room. Seeing no movement, she slipped quickly from the body to the side of the table and, gun braced in both hands, once again swept the interior of the barn for any sign of the second boarder.

There was no indication of life anywhere. The only sound was the continued slap, slap, slap of the cable line outside, the end of which Koski quickly ascertained was lying loose on the table, no longer hooked up to any of the deceased electronic devices.

Leaving the barn, she backtracked to enter the farmhouse. On entering the kitchen, it hit her: Crotchety Old Mr. Thorsdan was sitting in a kitchen chair on the other side of a square kitchen table, head thrown back, hands hanging down limply on either side of the chair. Behind him, the sink, cabinets and stove door were splattered with darkening blood and tissue. The man's face was staring wide-eyed directly towards heaven, having one, small, round, entry hole in the middle of his forehead. Koski did a quick search of the kitchen, but found nothing in there or in the adjacent living room that could shed any further light on what had happened. A careful examination of the rest of the house revealed nothing extraordinary.

Piecing together what she could, it seemed to her that whoever had shot the girl in the barn must have first shot Thorsdan. There being no signs of struggle on either body and the shots being delivered at very close range, it was likely that the shooter was known to each. That the barn table was only half loaded with "murdered" equipment suggested to Koski that some of the equipment had left the scene probably with the second houseguest, not long ago in the bay of the old, grey-primer-coated Ford. Her principal worry at the moment was if and when the shooter would return to pick up the rest of the equipment.

Satisfied she had extracted everything she could for the moment, Koski placed a call to the local police, and described the scene to the female policewoman who had earlier accompanied her to the Thorsdan farm, promising at the policewoman's insistence to return to her car and stay alert until help arrived. The officer assured her she would put out an All Points Bulletin for a Ford pickup driven by a young Oriental female.

Koski, however, did not return to her car as promised. Instead, she returned to the barn to examine more closely the equipment and the satellite dish.

The equipment was definitely exotic in nature. It all appeared custom made, some labels looking like they had been created with a Chinese-character label-maker and hastily stuck on. It would take an expert to figure out what each of the units was designed to do, and that would require alerting Cerebrus as soon as she checked out the antenna. She needed to give them as accurate and comprehensive a field description as possible.

Climbing a ladder into the loft, she opened the loft window to gain entrance to the roof and examine the antenna dish. In doing so, Koski noticed in the distance a set of headlights bobbing along the approach road. Given that there were no flashing red lights, she surmised it was the old Ford truck with the Oriental.

The antenna would have to wait. It was too late to hide her parked rental car. For now, the best she could do was to locate a secure place from which she could observe and, if necessary, defend herself against what was, by all accounts, an exceptionally dangerous, professional killer.

Chapter 19

The black, half-bed, crew-cab truck, it's six over-cab floodlights ripping through the darkness, jostled along the dirt side-road that led to the Jersey's. Stewart's teeth chattered as the truck barreled down the washboard road. Hitting a pothole, he and the Red River Militia flew into the air. Greyside, the driver and militia commander quickly ground the monster machine into low four-wheel drive to avoid losing further control and they plowed through the deeply muddied ruts that on the surface looked like long, narrow lakes of brackish black water.

"Hold on!" the commander yelled.

The next moment, Stewart, Frey, Smart and Lexington were again airborne, the latter three a mixture of flying limbs and weapons. Frey and Lexington seemed to be enjoying the moment. Smart, sitting between the two muscle-bound men, swore quietly to herself that she'd never travel with the

Keystone Cops again.

Stewart, despite the jostling, maintained his focus and concentration on his mission to investigate the isolated homestead from which the most recent event was calculated to have emanated.

"The Jersey place," a gritty male voice volunteered from behind Stewart, laying a hand on Stewart's left shoulder and pointing with the other to the right of the road where, outside of the cone of light from the headlights and over-cab floodlights, everything looked opaque black.

An instant later, Greyside snapped off all the lights, and brought the truck to a stop in front of what looked like two log cabins in the middle of a forest clearing.

"The Jerseys," the commander repeated, pointing at the closer of the two lightless cabins swallowed whole by the moonless night. "Macintosh Jersey, his wife, Elaine, an' those two foreign girls I told you about." Climbing out of the cab, he barked, "Frey! Lexington! You're with me. Smart! You're wing and point man, er, woman, for our government man here! I'm counting on you to make sure nothing bad happens to him!"

Wrapped entirely in black, the woman looked like a pair of floating, disembodied, demonic eyes against the background of darkness. Shifting on her seat, she snapped a clip into what Stewart had earlier identified as a frankly illegal, fully automatic, Russian-made assault rifle, then grunted.

In seconds, the three men had deployed soundlessly about the nearer cabin, weapons at ready. Stewart slid out of the truck with Smart, his "point-and-wing-woman" following several steps behind him. Crouching against a large tree trunk twenty-feet from the first cabin, Stewart paused to assess the situation.

The cabin's far windows were shuttered, but the ones to either side of the log door weren't, being only curtain-closed from the inside. There were no signs of life, but it was late at night and Stewart felt certain from the cabins' rustic appearance that the Jersey's didn't do much socializing after sunset.

As his eyes adjusted to the darkness, individual pinpoint of stars began to appear above him, then more and more, until the sky-dome above looked like it was splattered with bags of crushed diamonds, some running together into a swath of what truly looked like spilled milk. Living in Washington DC for over twenty years, he'd forgotten what the night sky looked like behind the constant hazy illumination produced by the nation's energetic capital. Following the outer rim of the Big Dipper constellation that pointed without fail to the North Star, he noticed below the pole star the dark nondescript outline of the smaller second cabin.

The presence of the smaller cabin emphasized the size of the larger, nearer one, it's expected silhouette broken by an exotic looking satellite dish pointing low to the horizon. *Interesting*, he was thinking, when a flash appeared in the corner of the window to the right of the first cabin's door. He heard a thup behind him, then a deafening report that echoed into every corner of the night. Looking behind, Stewart watched his point-and-wing-woman fall hard and lifeless onto the forest floor.

Before Stewart could call out to Greyside, all hell broke loose. Flashes, thumps and reports erupted from seemingly everywhere, a whiz of bullets surrounding him. Falling flat on the ground, he retrieved his automatic from his shoulder holster and was about to brace and fire when the flashes, whizzes, thumps and bangs all abruptly stopped.

Stewart waited, expecting to see the outline of Greyside, Frey or Lexington approach the cabin doors or creep back to the truck.

Neither occurred.

Instead, absolute darkness and quiet once again prevailed. Crawling backwards to where Smart had fallen, the head of Cerebrus felt her unmoving neck for a pulse. Finding none, he lay beside her and thought hard about what to do next.

There was no movement he could see inside or outside either cabin. The silence that had re-engulfed him was heightened by the sigh of the night wind working its way through the tops of nearby pines, including the one behind which he had crouched and then judiciously abandoned.

After what seemed hours but what was likely only minutes, Stewart began inching his way further behind the dead woman, hoping to use her body as a shield between himself and the cabins. Having accomplished the task, he called out, "Mr. and Mrs. Jersey—Macintosh! Elaine!—I don't know what just happened, but I'm a…a scientist with the…Montana State Department of Natural Resources," Stewart fabricated as he talked. "I was sent here to find out about a…freak electrical disturbance…reported to have occurred in this area."

Waiting patiently, hearing no answer and seeing no signs of movement, he allowed himself to shiver from the cold that was already penetrating his clothing, and continued with his *ad hoc* "explanation," hoping it would make just enough sense to whoever heard it to say something. Anything.

"I've been sent to make sure you and your boarders are okay."

Again, no reply. No sound or movement anywhere other than the now continuous sigh of cold night air working its way from the tops of the trees to where he was lying. Unable to think of anything further to say, Stewart decided to change tack. "Greyside! Frey! Lexington! Anybody!"

Again, no reply. Stewart slipped his cell phone out of his

pocket and speed-dialed Cerebrus headquarters. Immediately after the first buzz, a reassuring female voice answered: "The James' residence."

"Code five-four," Stewart answered, repeating it again a moment later as protocol required.

After a click and a brief pause, a male voice replied, "Is this an emergency, Sir?"

"I really don't know. There's been a firefight at Thunderbolt. I repeat, a firefight at Thunderbolt."

"Are you in need of assistance or extraction, Sir?"

"What I need is for you to direct an infrared eye over the area where I am and tell me what you see."

"Yes, Sir," came the immediate reply, and several minutes later, "We see one 'hot' life-form on the ground lying prone next to a 'cold' one…"

"The hot one would be me, the other, Smart, a militia woman who accompanied me here and was shot dead," Stewart interrupted.

"…with three more 'cold' lifeforms outside either end of two small wooden structures. Inside the structure nearest you there appear to be four more 'cold' lifeforms. Wait, one is only borderline 'cold'. It's hard to tell for sure when looking through a roof. There are none, 'hot' or 'cold', inside the structure furthest from you. Behind you is what looks to be an empty

SUV..."

"Thanks," Stewart interrupted. "That's all I needed. I'm going to inspect the first structure. I'll get back to you after that. Code five-four out."

Moments later, shoulder against the door of the first cabin, his body aligned to project the least possible target, Stewart called out several more times, each time receiving no response. Having sufficiently announced his presence in the most benevolent manner he could come up with, he gripped his automatic in his right hand and pressed his other hand hard against the door. The door swung open, and he called out a final time. Yet again, no answer.

He didn't enter, however.

Instead, after allowing his eyes to adjust to the even darker cabin interior, he peeked carefully from the lower corner of the doorway. "Mr. Jersey? Mrs. Jersey? My name is Stewart. I'm a representative of the Montana State Department of Natural Resources. I was asked to investigate an unusual electrical outage. I'm just checking to make sure you and your boarders are okay." It remained a flimsy explanation at best, but, as field protocol dictated, he would continue with it. "Mr. Jersey? Mrs. Jersey," he repeated, working his body slowly sidewise through the narrow doorway opening into the cabin.

The two now open-curtained windows on either side of the

door offered no light, but his eyes, having already become accustomed to darkness, he could vaguely make out a log cabin interior with sparse wood furnishings: a rough picnic table with attached benches on the far side of the cabin, a smoldering wood stove, a tin sink with a hand water pump. There were two open doorways on the far wall, each presumably leading to a bedroom. He could just make out two adult-sized bodies sitting at the picnic-table, each slumped awkwardly forward. On the floor between the wood stove and sink, next to an orderly stack of wood was a smaller unmoving body. Stewart couldn't make out any chest rise or fall. These would be the three "cold" bodies. So where was the…

A shadow moved out from the right bedroom doorway and disappeared behind the far side of the picnic table. Stewart crouched and braced his weapon, pointing it at the place where the shadow disappeared. "I didn't come here to hurt anyone. I'm here to check and make sure everyone is okay. If you'll just…"

Three flashes from behind the table were followed by the zing of three bullets passing immediately to his left. Stewart fell flat on the floor, re-braced his weapon and squeezed off two shots into the darkness just above where he suspected one of the two boarders to be hiding.

"Those were warning shots!" he yelled loudly. "Put down your weapon and let's talk…" He was interrupted by three more flashes in quick succession from behind the table, followed by three dull thuds in the wall where he'd been crouching a moment ago. Whoever it was had a small caliber semi-automatic pistol, assumedly the same Type 77 that the other Oriental agents had. Assuming it hadn't been reloaded, that left, at most, one bullet, in the chamber.

Stewart rolled silently to the side, re-braced and was about to speak again when, hearing the click of an ammunition clip being replaced, he sprang forward, gun leveled directly at the barely perceptible shadow-form in front of him. A quick sweep with his weapon-hand knocked the gun and two clips from his assailant's hands across the floor. Pointing his automatic between the whites of two youthful but scared Oriental looking eyes, he said, "It's over. I told you, I'm just here to help. Now stand. Slowly. I don't want to shoot, but I will if you make me."

The shaking figure slowly unraveled itself and stood before him revealing a very frightened Oriental youth in her early 20's, her narrow ferret-like eyes darting from Stewart to every object and corner of the room. Moving slowly to his left, Stewart picked up the impotent weapon and balanced it in his hand inspecting it with two quick glances. "Chinese made Type 77," he confirmed. As he spoke, the girl sprang towards the door, only to trip over Stewart's suddenly outstretched leg, and fall smartly face down onto the floor.

"We really need to talk," Stewart said, indicating with the barrel of his gun a lone wooden chair sitting against the far wall between the two open bedroom doors.

Chapter 20

"Talk," Stewart repeated firmly, but before she could begin, his cell phone interrupted.

The girl stared at Stewart, squirming uncomfortably, a desperate wildness in her eyes while he listened to the voice on the other end of his phone and watched her closely.

When Stewart signed off, he returned his full attention to his captive, beginning his field interrogation with a test of her English. "There's been…an electrical problem reported. I was sent here to make sure everyone was okay. I'm here to protect you. Do you understand? I'm here to protect…"

His question was cut short when her squirming abruptly stopped. Her body became rigid, and she pointed her chin haughtily up towards the rough-hewn ceiling.

"So you *do* understand me?" Stewart half-asked, half-stated. "Okay, let's start with a name. As I said, my name's Stewart. I'm here to protect you, but I need to know who you are and from what exactly I am protecting you. Can you tell me? Do you have a name?"

"Dah Choo-Tow," the girl replied icily.

"Is that your name?" Stewart asked.

"Dah Choo-Tow," the girl repeated.

"Okay, Dah Choo-Tow, I need to know what happened here."

"American mother, father, wake us. 'Soldiers outside,' they say. Mother and Father say, 'Go into bedroom.' We sit quiet on bed. We hear noise outside. Father Jersey, he get gun and shoot out window. Kill all soldiers but one, I think." The corners of Dah Choo-Tow's mouth thinned and her eyes widened as if reliving the event. "Soldier…he shoot Father, then Mother, then Mary. Try shoot me. I shoot him first." Tears began flowing.

Stewart was certain Dah Choo-Tow, if that was, in fact, her real name, was doing exactly what he had been doing a few moments ago while lying outside in the dirt using Smart's lifeless body as cover: constructing a cover story on-the-fly.

"I think not," Stewart replied, offering the girl a second chance.

"I…I…scared. Maybe happen different. Can't think. I guess…"

"I'm guessing that you're making this all up," Stewart interrupted, waving the handgun she had pointed at him only moments ago. "Let's start over and try again, beginning with this weapon."

The girl abruptly stopped crying. Her eyes narrowed and in the next instant she exploded from her seat, spinning and directing a heel, like lightening, at the center of Stewart's chest. The thud of the impact should have filled the room. Instead, Stewart reflexively thrust his gun arm forward, barely deflecting the foot-thrust, and, dropping both weapons, locked his fingers about the base of her wrist. With a twist, he knocked her off balance. The girl screamed in pain and fury.

"Let's start again," Stewart said, shaken, calmly picking his gun up from the floor while continuing to hold her wrist in the paralyzing one-handed Aikido hold.

The girl tried to struggle, but, realizing that even the smallest movement elicited incredible pain, immediately stopped. Acknowledging defeat, she relaxed. Stewart guided her back onto the chair. "So, once again, Dah Choo-Tow, I need to know what really was going on here."

A gust of wind rustled the leaves outside and rattled a window. The girl startled in her seat, a look of unbridled fear flushing her face. "I can not tell you that," she replied in perfect international English. "If I did, I would soon be as dead as they are," she said, inclining her head towards the bodies in the cabin. Continuing, in the same breath she said, "You can not protect me. Not now. No one can."

Stewart listened with growing interest. And concern.

"No one can!" she repeated more forcefully with a sob. Then after a pause, "Can you?"

"I don't know. I can't until I know what is going on, Dah Choo-Tow."

The girl paused as if thinking. "Dah Choo-Tow' means 'Die, Pig!" and, in another sudden burst of energy, she threw herself directly at Stewart. To his horror, he felt his gun ripped from his hand. The next moment, she placed its point in her mouth, and, before he could react, pulled the trigger.

The explosion was deafening. Her young body flew against the back of the chair.

"Damn!" he shouted to himself, realizing that the person he had been attempting to interrogate had been a highly-trained and utterly dedicated professional. Laying the limp form aside, he wiped the blood splatters from his hands onto his pants, searched for and located a lantern, lit it and began inspecting her and the other bodies in the room. All, it appeared, had met their death at the hands of an expert using the weapon he'd obtained from her, and she used on herself.

It was, then, she who killed everyone in the room, he mentally summarized.

Searching the room, he found two thirty-aught-six caliber

hunting rifles with military grade sniper scopes, one beneath each of the two open windows. Both had been recently fired based on the sharp smell emanating from their breaches. This was confirmed by the presence of twelve, large, empty casings littered about on the floor. Mr. Jersey's trigger finger and the right side of his face showed faint powder marks, presumably from firing one of the rifles. The same was true of the other girl, "Mary." Mr. and Mrs. Jersey, he surmised, had, in the end, in the process of "defending" themselves, somehow gotten in the way of whatever the two girls were up to.

From a cursory examination of the room, Stewart guessed that the Jersey's were indeed rural survivalists. They'd probably heard the SUV approach, and, for some reason, both Mr. Jersey and Mary, if that was indeed her real name, had donned rifles and began expertly picking off the militia and very nearly him. That strongly suggested that Mary was more than just a "farm girl from Nebraska." The incidents, in light of Mr. Jersey and the girls' behavior, elevated the events in Stewart's mind to acts of terrorism, and given that the Chinese girl had been the sole initial survivor, quite probably a carefully planned act perpetrated by China. Either way, he had to get in contact with the Joint Chiefs, Falk, Koski and Rellin, and return to Cerebrus headquarters as quickly as possible with the odd electrical equipment he'd noticed shoved haphazardly under one of the beds, and he needed to do it quickly. In that order. And now!

Chapter 21

Back in Washington DC, Cerebrus and NSA computer experts were working around-the-clock, nervously anticipating a fourth event, predicting that if the current pattern held, it would occur somewhere in western or central Washington state.

The large, multi-screen situation board displayed the three current event epicenters. About them were thousands of red dots. The dots ranged in diameter from pinpoints to half-inch, most individual but some amalgamated, the whole forming rings of concentric red circles about the event epicenters. The boldness of the dots and the lines reflected the number of deaths and injuries. Millions of softer grey points, representing unconfirmed reports of incidents created a disturbing surreal background. The current focus of this shift of analysts, computer specialists and electrical engineers wasn't so much on the three epicenters, however, or the rapidly growing and coalescing dots, as it was the points where the expanding rings intersected. Wherever event echo rings from separate events intersected, the resulting damage was far in excess of what each's diminishing power would predict.

While hotly arguing and re-arguing the physics of what they were observing and its implications regarding the nature of the originating events, the eastern portion of Washington state began pulsing a pale yellow, and a date-and-time stamp appeared in its upper right corner, indicating, based on accumulated information, the broad area-location of the anticipated fourth epicenter. The fact that they could predict and sound an area alert at all offered some small reassurance, and allowed area authorities to prepare. To everyone's consternation, Spokane was located in the exact center of the area alert. A vibrant city of 250,000, a major United States Air Force Strategic Air Command base was located less than twelve miles away.

As this realization sunk in, debate stopped. No one was willing to offer an opinion about what this might portend, but it was clear from the resulting murmurs that everyone was concerned that if the actual epicenter occurred in or anywhere near a large urban center like Spokane, the new event would likely demand application of all available city, state and federal resources. That would leave few available for the next event, which, if the pattern held, was already being predicted to occur in or around Seattle, Washington (unlikely, given the relatively short distance between Seattle and Spokane); San Francisco, Los Angeles, San Diego or Anchorage (again unlikely, as they would represent a significant North/South shift in direction); leaving Honolulu, Hawaii the most likely fifth epicenter.

Seconds later, a new flashing dot appeared, as feared, ten miles outside of Spokane, Washington. At the same time, reports began coming in regarding the presence of the anticipated auction, this time for possession of the Western non-coastal states. Though things were looking bleak, a cheer arose in the room when Colonel Rellin announced they'd finally narrowed down the auction source and some of the BitCoin bid locations and the albeit circuitous internet pathway being used. Both the previous and current auction were relayed through multiple complex networks of TOR-related Internet Service Providers, ISPs, scattered all over the world. The initial sell offer, it was back-calculated, had most likely originated from somewhere near the Russian/Chinese/North Korean border. Bids had originated from hundreds of different areas around the world, the exact points of origin of all of the bids still being determined. With this information in hand, Rellin's experts could now state with certainty that three times a major financial exchange had indeed taken place, and with the anticipated fourth transaction, the absurdity of "buying" regions of the USA had reluctantly congealed into a still formless but overarching fear of, when all the transactions were completed, what would be the result and its additive effect.

It was at this point Colonel Rellin excused himself to take two urgent phone calls first, from the Chairman of the Joint Chiefs of Staff, and then, on hold, from Cerebrus field agent Joseph Falk.

Chapter 22

Stewart's first call had been to General Richard Cavors, the tall, aloof, acerbic Chairman of the Joint Chiefs of Staff. General Cavors received Stewart's information politely and respectfully, but with audible disbelief. There wasn't time for Stewart to ask why, but it seemed likely it involved the General being privy to information he was reticent to share at this time.

Disappointed but nonplussed, Stewart, like all players in an ascending "need to know" organization, accepted the situation for what it was, trusting General Cavors would share what he, Stewart, had provided with the other chiefs of staff, and would, when appropriate, share back with Cerebrus the apparently restricted information to which Cavors alone was apparently privy.

Next he called Falk, Falk's site being the first, and Falk having had the most time to investigate. What Stewart heard was troubling.

"Falk," his number one Cerebrus agent answered.

"Report, Joe," Stewart ordered.

"Not good, sir. When I returned to the Hempsted farm, I found Aaron Hempsted in the living room, a bullet through his head. It was a professional job. I searched upstairs for the two female boarders, and heard a scream followed by gunshots. A young Caucasian girl had been killed, or rather, executed, in the same way as Aaron Hempsted. The second, a young Asian girl, supposedly the murderer, shot herself before I could stop her."

"God Almighty!" Stewart exclaimed, shocked at how similar their investigative field experiences had been. "Any suggestion of what they were up to? Any idea how this might relate to the events and auctions? And any idea if the satellite dish you mentioned might be involved?"

"I'm going on the assumption my two girls worked as a team," Falk replied. "The Asian's weapon was an older Chinese-made, 7.62 millimeter Type 77 semi-automatic, the preferred weapon some years ago of the Chinese intelligence community. I'm again assuming she murdered Hempsted, then her partner, then, being the leader and surprised by me, shot herself to avoid being taken and interrogated. What she would have done had I not surprised her, and where she would have gone afterwards are, at this point, pure conjecture; however,

I'm going to guess her next action would have been to destroy what looks like a number of very unusual custom-made receivers that I found in their room. All are physically inter-connected, the whole being attached by a wire to the outside satellite dish.

"There were no commercial marks on the equipment or the dish, although there are some labels written in what appears to be Chinese" he continued. "As I said, both equipment and antenna appear custom-made. Looking over the equipment, my best guess is that it represents some kind of advanced EMF generator. Except, of course, that wouldn't fit what we're seeing in terms of the 'echoes'. No, not an EMF generator. Something different. Something incredibly more sophisticated. The receivers, if that's what they are and antenna look quite complex, and I'm guessing that the core electronics are distributed between the units and antenna. That is, they are integral parts of a single device, making it difficult for someone acquiring any one part to ascertain the actual manner in which the event was generated. It all smacks of a very sophisticated job by the Chinese, or by someone using Chinese-made or, at the least, Chinese acquired resources. Alternatively, they could be meant to *implicate* the Chinese…"

"Make arrangements to ship everything to Cerebrus," Stewart said, "and I'll call in our best electronic geniuses. By the way, how do you think the Chinese and whoever else is behind this got hold of this kind of technology when *we* don't have it? Or do we?" Stewart continued, thinking out loud about General Cavors' reluctance to share, and, after a pause, adding, "Koski is investigating at the second event epicenter..."

"The Asian was a professional. Tell Koski..."

"I'll notify her immediately," Stewart interrupted. "In the meantime, as I said, package up the equipment, including the unusual antenna, and have it all sent to Cerebrus Ops Central and notify Colonel Rellin when it's on its way. By the time the equipment gets here, General Cavors of the Joint Chiefs of Staff will have advised him of what we've collectively found and ordered Rellin and our staff to figure out some way to defend against this technology."

Stewart clicked off and speed-dialed Koski. What he heard was even more disturbing.

"Koski," came the familiar female voice on the other end of the connection.

"Stewart here. I've just talked with Falk. I need your report."

"Is he..."

"Yes," Stewart responded with audible compassion. "He's fine." In the momentary pause, Stewart heard Koski let out a soft sigh. "But I need to know everything you've found out,

Susan. Now!"

"On a tip from an anxious hotel waiter, I revisited the Thorsdan farm. I knew there was something wrong when I saw bales of hay I had noticed before in the back of an old pickup truck dropped haphazardly into the mud, and no truck. No farmer would leave stockfeed laying in the mud like that.

"I decided to check out the barn's satellite antenna like Falk indicated he was planning to do in Laplacia. Walking alongside what appeared to be a deserted barn, I located the cable running through a crack in siding. Inside the barn was a table covered with a number of interconnected electronic boxes. The equipment looked handmade and the labels appeared to be in Chinese. On closer inspection, each unit was heavily damaged, shot through several times. It also appeared from a number of clean 'squares' on the tabletop that half of the equipment was gone. In the center of the floor was a tall, thin, Caucasian girl. She'd been shot once in the forehead and a second time from behind. All very professional."

Koski paused a moment to regain her composure and force the image of the girl's devastated face from her mind.

"I left the barn and checked out the farm house. There I found Thorsdan tied to a chair, killed in a similar manner. The second girl wasn't there. Assuming the frightened hotel waiter's description correct, she's a short, black-haired Oriental. I'm guessing she's using the truck to dispose of the equipment. I called the local police, then climbed up onto the barn roof to check out the antenna as I'd originally intended. While doing so, the truck returned, presumably to pick up the rest of damaged equipment."

Again Koski paused.

"And?" Stewart asked impatiently.

"I tried to capture her, but the moment she saw me running towards the truck, she shot herself."

Chapter 23

"Sir?" asked Colonel Rellin, holding the receiver of the "red" landline phone stiffly to his ear as if listening and saluting the voice on the other end of the line. General Richard Cavors, the Chairman of the United States' Joint Chiefs of Staff "humpfed" in confirmation. Cavors had just finished updating him on the information he'd received from Stewart, and informed the NSA liaison officer in no uncertain terms that it was absolutely necessary to expedite things or there'd soon be no reason left to do so.

"Our military and civilian resources are being rapidly exhausted," Cavors warned. "Civil unrest is on the rise, to the point of anarchy in some regions. An hour from now, the President will announce nation-wide martial law. Our most immediate problem, however, is we still haven't come up with an effective military response. Basically, no one has yet claimed responsibility for the situation. In short, there's no one for us to defend against or fight except our own citizens!"

"Sir. Are you saying the President is about to declare a state of 'war' against an unidentified enemy?" Colonel Mike Rellin asked, eyes widening, lines of worry cutting into his usually boyish face.

"Immediately after the first event," Cavors continued in a strained voice, "the President tasked my group with determining the endgame behind these 'events' and 'auctions'. Unfortunately, my colleagues and I still can't agree whether what's going on constitutes an 'untoward technical phenomena', a 'new kind of hack,' a 'malicious, coordinated terrorist attack' a prelude to war or an actual act of war, and, if the latter, by whom, how and why. The older, more persuasive members are certain our long time 'enemy', Russia, is somehow behind it all and are talking of advising the President to consider a tactical pre-emptive nuclear strike against Russia before our nuclear arsenal becomes inoperative."

"Russia?" echoed Rellin hollowly, stunned that the Joint Chiefs would perseverate on Russia, and that they were considering a "nuclear solution" with all that would likely encompass, not just for the two warring countries, but the entire world. "Has everyone gone crazy?" Rellin asked.

"Careful, Colonel. That kind of remark might be taken by someone other than me as insubordination or even outright treason. Most of my chiefs see today's world as an extension of the cold war turned hot. You've got to remember, they're from the 1960s through the 1990s and have seen Russia repeatedly act the master puppeteer. An hour ago they were arguing whether a tactical nuclear response even *could* stop the events, and whether we would be remembered by the world as defenders or aggressors. I don't share their opinion about Russia, and the longer I listen, the more I fear that if I can't identify who's really behind it and fast, Russia will by default become the enemy. It doesn't help that we've had no word—no word at all—from the Russians. One chief suggests they're trying to force America into the same kind of *perestroika/ glasnost* situation the former Soviet Union faced before breaking up. It seems like nothing would please their current President, the ruling party, military and regional moguls more than to see the United States of America dissolve into pieces like the former Soviet Union did."

"An American 'restructuring'," murmered Rellin, stunned even further. "It does make an odd sort of sense. Our nation has been torn these past years by one after another reactionary splinter group attempting to foist their way of thinking on the public as a whole. Whether one calls it the a Conservative revival, the re-emergence of the 'Old Southern Confederacy', 'White Supremacy,' 'Fascism' or a 'Second American

Revolution', it's a reflection of a nation being forced to redefine itself. Are the Joint Chiefs thinking that a consortium of disaffected American splinter groups with or without the assistance of organized crime might be behind these phenomena, with Russia behind them?"

The line fell silent in Rellin's hand. General Cavors, obviously not wanting to go there, replied instead, "Unless your group can clarify the source of the threat, or at least come up with an effective defense against these 'events', Russia, I'm afraid, will very soon cease to exist, and, in its wake, possibly the entire civilized world."

"That's a heavy responsibility to place on my people, Sir. We've been working around the clock in a co-ordinated, inter-agency effort to do just that."

"And...?"

"The shared thinking here *at the moment*," he ventured cautiously, "is that it might actually be China rather than Russia."

"China?" asked Cavors in a flat voice. "A nation of workers led by a business-suited Communist bureaucracy? A nation so out of touch with its people, it no longer knows what's going on within its nation and its people? No, The Joint Chiefs wouldn't buy that China has sufficient interest at this time in covertly planning and launching such a dangerous operation, or having at its disposal the advanced technology that's being employed here. Hell, in their mind, China's leaders are on the verge of becoming rich, just like ours. You might better invoke the 'Big Conspiracy Theory' that everyone, inside and outside the USA, who, for one reason or another, hates us or what we stand for, is secretly colluding to bring us down. Listen, Rellin, if there's one task the United States has been consistently good at over the years, it's intelligence gathering, and there's been nothing on the 'whisper network' indicative of any kind of Chinese conspiracy real or shadow. No, the Joint Chiefs think it's got to be Russia. As far as the observation that most of the equipment you've gathered has labels in Chinese, and the *agents provocateur* are of Oriental extraction, the Joint Chiefs think it's all just too obvious. It's so obvious, they think it's more likely Russia framing China. Our current thinking is that Russia would benefit both directly and indirectly from a war between us and China, irrespective of who 'wins.'"

"So…?" Colonel Rellin asked.

"So, I need you to ramp up your efforts and *prove* it is or isn't Russia, so we will have someone concrete to fight. If you don't, and I mean soon, my group will certainly lay the blame on Russia and recommend initiating plans to…"

"I understand," Rellin replied with determined finality. "Every agency here will do what's necessary to work the problem and get you the answer you need."

Chapter 24

Stewart's dead captive hadn't provided her real name. Or her mission. Or for whom she was working. He had obviously interrupted her while she was trying to clean up after the event that had occurred in the cabin in the woods just before the militia and he arrived. Even so, despite the briefness of the interrogation, he'd noted the Chinese weapon she was carrying, and, was certain, despite her perfect Chinese, from the inflection of her voice, she was not really Chinese. From what little she'd said, she sounded to him more Korean than Chinese. Invoking his linguistic skills, he would say North Korean, if he had to hazard a guess.

As much as he wanted to, he knew he couldn't safely conclude anything just yet. A Chinese weapon, while suspicious, didn't *guarantee* that the Chinese were behind any of what was going on. The Type-77 was an old issue and while still in use by some Chinese foreign agents, was no longer standard issue, having been replaced by the larger magazine, 9 millimeter QSZ-92 Type 92 semi-automatic. The gun could be a plant. And international spy agencies today typically recruited potential agents to fit specific requirements for a specific action. Even if she was Chinese or North Korean, that wasn't sufficient to implicate either. Worse yet, her North Korean roots could be a ploy by China to misdirect attention *away* from it and towards North Korea. No, he couldn't directly implicate anyone. Not yet.

On the other hand, in the bigger scheme of things, unlike the heated *military* encounters that were recurring between the United States and Russia throughout the world, *tensions* between China and the United States were always smoldering despite one after another "goodwill" gesture or cooperative agreement. And as for North Korea, it seemed be forever verbally provoking the United States and its partners, trying to goad them into action, and recently, this had become increasingly so. With the announcement of new and ever stricter United States initiated and supported sanctions, North Korea's usual hyperbole had escalated to venomous threats of mass destruction.

Still, the public was constantly being reminded on the hourly news of the increasing number and severity of Russian 'interventions' throughout the world. Was it any wonder then that top level military strategists were inclined to conclude that Russia was secretly attempting to resurrect a new USSR, or worse, in retribution, attempting to force the USA into a *perestroika/glasnost* of it's own? Such constant, high-visibility altercations could also serve as perfect cover distractions for China, or North Korea for that matter, to advance their own secret agendas. Also, since the United States had became more and more embroiled in containing Russian-supported insurgencies throughout the world, US and NATO alert levels had successively increased, with Russia following suit, most likely with China secretly laughing while North Korea egged all three nations on from behind.

Irrespective of who or what was behind the events and auctions and why, it was evident to Stewart that the three dead "Oriental" girls and their three American assistants or girlfriends were part of a larger cohesive plan. That the Oriental's role was significant could be deduced from the fact that their American "helpers" were, from the beginning, expendable. The Oriental he'd encountered knew something important, or she wouldn't have been so frightened of his offer of protection. What had she said? "You can not protect me. No one can." That suggested that they had handlers or supervisors probably located not far away. The capture of a handler, supervisor or even a live Oriental agent if possible had to become Stewart's new priority.

General profiles describing two female "students," one Oriental, the other Caucasian, boarding with an elderly American whose house had a new or "unusual" satellite antenna, were sent to all agency representatives converging on the predicted next event site along with a warning that the girls were to be assumed armed, dangerous and quite willing to kill. That said, it was of highest priority to capture rather than kill them and anyone in any way associated with them for further interrogation.

"What news?" asked an exhausted looking Stewart of Cerebrus' current shift Information Control Officer, after having returned from Montana.

"So far, nothing more," the equally exhausted Information Officer replied. "You're aware that the equipment you sent went down with the plane?"

"Wha...?" began Stewart.

"The Faraday cages didn't work. Apparently you were lucky to get there and back alive. Still, we have the equipment sent to us by your two agents, and, despite the equipment being custom-designed, and some of it being missing and some of it having been shot through several times, we're slowly piecing them together an aggregate whole."

"We don't have much time," Stewart half-thought, half-replied, sifting in his mind every bit of information he'd thus far gleaned. His best efforts unfortunately continued to refuse to yield anything actionable.

What he did know at this point was that it wasn't the events, but the fluid intersections of event-echoes that were doing the most damage, and that their number continued increasing. Every added event carried with it the promise of a massive number of new potential intersections. The more intersections, the more damage, with no upper limit in sight.

Two events created a predictable intersection pattern, three, within hours, required the best supercomputers the United States to predict intersections and issue warning to the citizenry. Add the fourth event and there were so many possible intersections that neither time nor sufficient computer resources existed to handle all the data. Within hours of the fourth event, even the resources of the most powerful, multiplexed, military/civilian computing facilities would be exceeded. The bottom line was that the events had now assumed the character of an all-out cyber and quite possibly physical attack. One like no other. And after a fifth event? Who knew?

That the primary target was United States was now also blatantly clear. There was no question either as to whether the intersections would eventually involve other countries. They were already affecting Canada *and* Mexico, though, of course, it wasn't yet clear if they represented collateral damage. Whether the events or intersections would spread to South America, Europe and Africa wasn't yet known. If Stewart's worse-case scenario were correct, in the end, not just the United States, but the entire Americas and perhaps even the majority of the world's nations would be brought to their knees. And who would be exempt? Who would benefit from global chaos and be willing to risk a global retaliatory attack? Who? And why?

There also remained the unsettling question of who was buying up the different geographic regions of the USA, and more importantly, who was selling, and why.

That the seller would amass a fortune was evident. Then there was the unthinkable question if whether the escalating events and intersections might not themselves be a distraction, a red herring, a rehearsal or means to "soften" the nation, predicating something even more deadly. The rapidly spreading sense of helplessness and panic that was sweeping the United States was proving an effective form of psychological warfare, if that's what it was meant to be. Add to that the specter of losing one's political identity to unknown aggressors, and the Blitzkreig of World War II, and nuclear threats of the 1960s and 70s paled in comparison. If the situation wasn't addressed soon, there'd be, as Rellin quoted General Richard Cavors, "nothing left to address."

One promising lead was that the events seemed connected to the equipment and satellite antennas that he, Falk and Koski had each noted at their respective sites. Sufficient equipment had reached Cerebrus' and NSA's joint technical expert teams to quickly determine that they weren't, in fact, of purely Chinese design and manufacture. Various components had come from a variety of countries, some even from the USA. More important, however, was what continued to elude the best minds Cerebrus had at its command, namely, the manner in which the equipment generated the events. The equipment was complex and immensely sophisticated, with its components distributed over many boxes. The two sets of equipment, while similar proved slightly different. Being hand-made, each set was probably designed for one use, and seemed more and more likely to be dedicated to the establishment of a unique two-way link for only a fraction of a second before shutting down entirely. To make things worse, electronic "red herrings" had been cleverly distributed throughout the system alongside auto-meltdown sections, the whole being designed to prevent anyone from extracting the technology involved. And it didn't help that neither of the groups of surviving equipment were complete, and that much of what they did have was partial, piecemeal or had been severely damaged.

Experts were frenetically trying to piece together parts from the two different systems to create a single functional system in hopes of gleaning what, if anything, could be done to stop, counteract or at least mitigate the events and their echo-effects.

The key, Stewart's Cerebrus' experts confided, was understanding the physics. While the purpose of the events and auctions, the critical "why" remained elusive and, at best, speculative, after sifting through the debris, all agreed that the event and echoes were indeed the result of a quantum effect, exploiting a quirk of quantum physics. That the quirk, whatever it was, caused destruction and death added to their increasingly popular attribution of the instruments being harbingers of "quantum death," which the overall operation had come to be labeled.

Separately extrapolating from Koski, Falk's and now the Washington equipment, it was possible for Cerebrus to calculate based on the direction each of the antennas had been oriented, a single point above Earth from which the incoming "start" signal would likely have originated. The problem was, they hadn't been all directed at a single point in space, and extrapolating, there was nothing located at the most likely point. Nothing! The assumption had been they would find a small, previously unnoticed geosynchronous satellite located at that point and would need only identify its owner to figure out who was at least behind the events. That assumption, however, had been proven incorrect. There was nothing anywhere near the predicted point except empty space.

Stewart left the Operations Room to attend a multi-agency update. After the lengthy briefing that disclosed nothing more than the current estimates as to the time and location of the next event, Stewart called Falk again.

"Falk," the voice on the other end answered.

"Stewart," he replied. "Have you got anything more for me?"

"Negative," Falk replied. "I've questioned everyone in town, but no one knows how the two girls ended up at old man Hempsted's. Their choice of hosts, however, couldn't have been better: He was an irascible old recluse, and pretty much avoided everyone."

"Any indication at all," Stewart asked, "if someone might have been waiting to spirit the Oriental girl away? It seems likely she would have had valuable field information to bring back to her controllers after the event. If nothing else, she would have had names, descriptions or locations of her controllers. Clearly the lead field agent was important, given that not one hesitated to take her life after eliminating everyone else associated with the event. I guessed there must be one or more nearby collaborators when I offered protection and the agent I was interrogating replied, 'You can not protect me. No one can.' It's a far shot, but…"

"Sorry to interrupt," Falk said, "but I've already 'been there, done that'. There's no indication whatsoever at this site that there were any other new or unusual additions to the area other than the two girls, or that they had consistent contact with anyone other than their host."

"Then I want you on the next available flight to Honolulu. Everything points to Honolulu being the next event site. I want you to oversee the various agencies while you do some snooping on your own. If there is one place where an agent provocateur could be most easily smuggled in and later out, it would be Hawaii with it's distinctly 'rainbow' population. See if you can come up with something. Report anything suspicious. Anything at all."

"Right," Falk acknowledged, adding, "Civilian air travel's a mess. Is the military still able to predict intersections enough to give a military pilot enough warning to avoid them? Most of the intersections, anyway. Can you ask Rellin to divert something military to Laplacia airport?"

"'Been there, done that'," Stewart replied. "Drive to the Laplacia airport and be waiting on the tarmac in half an hour."

After contacting Colonel Rellin and arranging for Falk's

flight, Stewart turned his attention to Koski.

"Koski here."

"Stewart, here," he replied. "Anything new?"

"Nothing," Koski replied, tiredness and frustration permeating her voice. "I've passed on everything like you ordered to Colonel Rellin. I interviewed Josh, the waiter I told you about who slipped me the note. For a seventeen-year-old, he was an excellent observer and quite the talker." Koski cleared her throat, thinking about the young waiter hitting on her. "Thorsdan was, like he said, his *honorary* not his real uncle."

The two paused for a moment, taking in the implications.

"Anything else?" Stewart finally asked.

"Aside from Josh's assessment that the two girls were possibly lovers, neither having responded to his advances…"

"Anything *pertinent*?" Stewart snapped.

"Sorry. Not really," Koski replied, angered by men constantly interrupting her. "The two girls kept pretty much to themselves and the townsfolk didn't go out of their way to inquire about them, which, now that I think of it, in itself seems unusual. People in small towns are usually quite interested in outsiders. Come to think of it, Josh, while talkative, has always seemed cautious, even fearful, as if concerned someone might overhear him. I need to go make some additional inquires."

"Be careful, Koski. According to our newest scenario, the agents might have one or more local handlers—someone watching them to make certain they carry out their assignments, and after completion, perhaps extracting, even eliminating the principal field agent. There's also the possibility of the handler being under the thumb of a near-site operations controller. If my hunch is correct, the two would likely be inconspicuous. People who had been there 'forever'. Persons I'd expect who would quietly disappear soon after the event was completed, with or without the principal agent."

"So you're calling them 'agents', now?" Koski mentioned. "Agents of…?"

"Everything ostensibly points to China, but I'm beginning to think that this may represent an ruse to put us off the trail of the real culprits. I strongly believe the 'Chinese' agent I tried to salvage and interrogate was actually of North Korean extraction."

"North Korean?" Koski reiterated, a distinct note of question in her voice. "Stewart! Wait a moment!"

Stewart overheard hurried but muffled talk on the other end of the line. "Our young Josh has disappeared! I've just ordered an areawide search for him."

"Consider him armed and *very* dangerous…"

"What about Falk?" Koski interrupted. "Anything new?

Has he identified a handler or controller? How…how is he?" The concern in her voice was palpable.

"He's fine. Nothing new in Laplacia. I'm sending him to Honolulu to see if there's a way to somehow nip in the bud what otherwise promises be the next event."

"By air?" Koski asked plaintively. Hearing no reply, she asked again, "By air, Stewart? I barely escaped death when an intersection passed over my *car*. The highway was left in chaos. While flying here, I had a…premonition…I mean, our air transportation system is unraveling…isn't there any way of protecting…?"

"Well, we tried Faraday cages, but have since learned they don't work against this…whatever it is. My plane was rigged with Faraday cages, and though my flight to Montana was uneventful, the plane carrying the site equipment never made it back. However, I'm informed that the military still have the capacity to compute, predict and avoid intersections. I sent him a military plane, like I'm sending you…"

"Wait! Me? But I've got Josh to locate and…"

"By now, I suspect your Josh, whether he was a handler, or controller or either attempting to turn informer will already be dead or long gone. I've issued an order to deploy another agent to Fulton to pick up where you leave off. I'll inform him regarding the young man. I want you at the Fulton airport, on the tarmac, ready to leave in twenty minutes. Go!"

Colonel Rellin was less affable when he received another military air transportation request. Stewart, in the meantime, decided to turn his attention to the enigmatic BitCoin auction and why, in light of the latest information, it was associated so closely with the events. One thing was clear: If China or North Korea was involved, it wouldn't be anything pleasant.

Chapter 25

Stewart grabbed the nearest Cerebrus officer. "Drop what you're doing and come with me. I'm calling a Tiger Team! Assemble our best in the conference room. Now! The meeting begins in ten minutes."

Exactly ten minutes later, nine harried looking men and women were choosing a seat around a large conference table.

"'Rocket fuel', anyone?" offered Stewart, holding up a glass pot filled with steaming, black, viscous coffee in one hand and a stack of styrofoam cups in the other. After accommodating the few takers, he replaced the pot on its heating pad and began.

"Thank you, ladies and gentlemen. I've called this Tiger Team to come to a consensus regarding the current situation. Whatever is happening is admittedly still in evolution, and while a pattern is emerging, the endgame is as yet not apparent. In the meantime, the world as we know it is spinning out of control. General Cavors, Chairman of the Joint Chiefs of Staff has conveyed to us an ultimatum: Identify the perpetrators *now* while our military resources are intact and we still can still mount a response."

Cerebrus' lanky Programs Manager, Franklin Gaston, second in command behind Stewart, shifted uneasily in his seat. "I fear there are at least as many theories floating about as to what's going on and who's behind it, Stewart, as there are persons around this table. How can you expect a consensus where there isn't any? Given what little we as yet individually and collectively know, I don't even see how a relevant consensus is possible."

"Good point, Franklin," replied Stewart. "Even so, as I said, it's soon going to become impossible for our nation to respond at all. According to General Cavors, we're losing this 'war,' if that's what it is, even as we talk. To defend our nation, we need to come to a common understanding regarding who is…"

"Isn't th…that your job, chief?" interrupted Dr. Jerry Falmouth, Cerebrus' Chief of Information Analysis.

"It would be, Jerry, if I had an understanding I could trust," replied Stewart. "As it happens, I have a guess, but it's as yet little more than that. Everything's happening so fast my 'guess' is hampered by our shared inability to keep up with all the incoming information. I might as well be wearing blinders. The situation continues to unfold too furiously to trust what any one person can construct in terms of a reliable or even reasonable overview. Everyone here's been concentrating on the evolving situation from his or her unique perspective. I assume we each have information we haven't yet had time to share, and a perspective that everyone else doesn't. If we pool what we know and what we suspect, I believe we might be able to come to a working consensus…"

"C…Consensus?" repeated Falmouth. "Is that r…really enough for the Joint Ch…Chiefs to concoct an effective response?"

"Another good point, Jerry," Stewart acknowledged. "In the mid-1960s, the United States was faced with a not dissimilar problem: It was impossible to know the former Soviet Union's tactical nuclear response to various situations with any certainty, so the government contracted a then deep-cover 'think-tank' to invent a method to force consensus. What resulted was the 'Delphi Technique'. It didn't result in a complete or perfectly valid understanding of the former USSR's most likely tactical nuclear responses, but it was good enough to allow us to create a response plan that later proved sufficiently effective. I propose applying this technique here, now, so we will come to a consensus that we can offer the Joint Chiefs to help them decide what to do.

"Like each of you, I've been sifting through everything I know again and again, attempting to assemble it into something cohesive and meaningful with which to work. Everyone here, I know, has been doing the same. I believe it's time to share with each other all we know as of this moment, and our best guesses as to what is going on. Applying the Delphi Technique should help bring us all to a consensus."

"How much time will this take? Things are evolving pretty rapidly and each of us needs to stay on top of his or her respective areas," inquired David Hallard, Cerebrus' normally dashing but currently harried-looking Head of Field Operations. "I'm responsible for directing unfolding operations in multiple locations which are continuing to emerge as we speak."

"Then let's limit ourselves to five minutes each to summarize what we've each uncovered and have concluded thus far from our respective points of view," Stewart recommended. "I'm familiar with Delphi. I'll lead us through it."

"Interruptions?" inquired Hallard, clearly concerned about diverting *any* of his attention away from field operations.

"Permitted, as the situation continues to unfold," answered Stewart. "We have, unfortunately, little time before the next event. Shall we begin?"

"I'll start," offered Kate Keenan, Cerebrus' new Chief Scientist and Technical Advisor, an acknowledged physics genius and computer wizard. "I've been investigating the details of the events, and who in the world would have the technical knowledge and resources to pull them off."

"Good," interrupted Stewart. "So…?"

"These days, practically any nation, multi-national corporation, rogue state or criminal organization could scrape together the necessary logistical *resources*. Few, however, would have the knowledge to understand, apply and manage the whole. The effects of the *events* seem straightforward, so I've had my group focus on the 'auctions', the effects of which are anything but. Specifically, I've been attempting to trace the path of the BitCoin transactions.

"I've come to the conclusion that it's more beneficial to determine who would have the *desire* or, restated, *be desperate enough* to try an auction like this. The key, I think, is identifying which of the many groups would stand to gain the most from such a gamble, and a big gamble it is.

"That the 'events' and 'auctions' are related seems incontrovertible. And, while the *who* and *how* are both necessary, our immediate need remains to ascertain the *why*.

"From this," Keenan concluded, "should come the who and how."

Stewart nodded in agreement. Several other participants around the table shook their heads, some in agreement, others in disagreement. It was clearly hard for anyone at the table to imagine a single entity in this intricately interconnected world of global economic and military *detante* that would have the audacity to risk total financial excommunication or physical obliteration for *any* end. Yet, if Kate was right, and it appeared to Stewart and many about the table that Cerebrus' technical genius was at the least on the right track, and that that was exactly what whoever was behind it was doing.

"Okay. Any ideas as to…?" Stewart began.

"Nothing certain," piped up David Hallard, Cerebrus' Head of Field Operations, stimulated by Kate Keenan's analysis and the freedom they were being given to express themselves. "If it were a nation, my money would have to be on North Korea. They, more than any other nation, have the need, desire, and, given their current state of affairs, the most to gain if successful as well as the least to lose should it prove, in the end, unsuccessful.

"A multi-national corporation? Name practically any global corporation, and it's *possible*. It's not that big a step from manipulating national economies using financial derivatives to fielding these auctions. Add to that, business ethics have, for years, been on a fast slippery slope. If it were a multi-national corporation, and I had to bet on one today, it would be SysGen. Tomorrow, who knows?

"As for a rogue state, any number of emerging, hyper-religious, xenophobic, terrorist 'states' would fit the bill. However, none have stepped forward to claim responsibility, so this situation, in my opinion, doesn't have the usual 'terrorist' ring to it. What we're experiencing seems darker, more organized and secular. If this were the brainchild of a rogue terrorist state, my bet, and it would be a poor one, would have to be the Islamic State of Iraq and the Levant—ISIS.

"There are currently several global *criminal* organizations that might have the interest and desire, but I imagine them to be the buyers rather than the seller or organizer."

"A...Agreed," interjected Falmouth. As the attention of everyone sitting around the conference table shifted back to Falmouth, Stewart, Keenan and Hallard relaxed back in their seats. "As K...Kate said, the key is *p...purpose*. Nonetheless, my group's work has been t...tightly focused not on p... purpose, but who was b...buying."

"And...?" Stewart asked.

"The buying seems highly c...competitive. That makes me th...think the bidders represent d...different groups. They could conceivably represent a c...consortium of anti-American nations and organizations, bidding one against the other for various 't...territories'. Spheres of influence. If so, each would have it's own r...reason and m...motive. Their principal commonalities would be, first, a long-standing d...desire to 'open up' the United States to global organized c...crime; second, their having sufficient monetary r...resources to 'compete' in an auction of this scope; th...third, there being an interest in obtaining wh...what amounts to the 'rights' to control a particular r...region of the United States."

"What about China, Jerry?" Stewart asked, reflecting on the Chinese labels on some of the recovered equipment.

"Ch...China?" Falmouth asked. "The equipment c... collected from each event site so far has 'Ch...China' written all over it. But, no, I can't see China b...behind these auctions. It would be easier for them to simply 'b...buy' the United States outright than to engage in a s...secret cyber-war with all-out, nuclear war a likely result. Any war between the US and Ch... China, would have an uncertain outcome, at best. Also, a global holocaust would destroy the very r...resources that China so c...covets. Besides Ch...China is heavily invested in the USA. Hell, they p...practically own America's debt. If China *were* behind this, it would be like attacking itself. If for that reason alone, China, in my opinion, w...wouldn't likely be the organizer, despite the obvious s...signs. A covert 'helper' perhaps, or the dupe, but the p...principal instigator? I don't think so."

"If I catch your drift, Jerry," Stewart replied, "China, in effect, already controls our resources and market simply by virtue of holding the mass of our national debt. Calling in the debt and publicly lording it over us in front of thc would be easier and more 'Chinese-style' than this.

"Y…Yes," Falmouth agreed excitedly. "Any organized, combined cyber-physical-economic attack against the USA, wh…which this is quickly becoming, w…would also, by d… definition, seriously effect China. Already the events and echo-intersections, though so far restricted to the USA, southern C… Canada and northern M…Mexico, are sending shock waves not just through our nation but th…through our allies as well as our adversaries, b…because we're all so economically dependent on each other. Irrespective of the instigator, the events seem to be p…pointing towards a f…final coordinated strike. Even if Ch…China *had* the means—and I'm not saying it d…does—if what I know is correct, it has no m…motive. And as to p… purpose, why make their participation so obvious by leaving Ch…Chinese labels on the field equipment? Ineptitude? No, the labels have the distinctive feel of a r…red herring…"

"If not China, then who?" asked Stewart.

"W…why not North Korea?" Falmouth half-asked, half-replied.

"How about you, Bob? What have you eked out from your group's global strategic analyses? What's your idea about who's behind the events and auctions?" Stewart asked, shifting the group's attention to Robert Small, the diminutive but brilliant Head of Cerebrus' Gobal Strategic Analysis Division, who, for an outspoken man, had thus far remained unusually silent.

"Huh?" Robert asked as if startled back to reality. "Sorry, I was considering whether the event epicenters and auction items would remain in the continental USA, or, if the next one did indeed occur in Honolulu, what the impact would be on the Pacific Rim nations. It seems like it would, in effect, bring them all down with us. Both events and auctions have thus far been confined to the continental USA." Robert Small, having shared, appeared to retreat back into his thoughts.

"I'm having serious reservations about the whole China-North Korea-Hawaii thing," stated Lou Richards, Cerebrus' Head of External Security, the youngest of the individuals around the table.

"Perhaps you'd share your concerns, Lou, and shed some light on who you think might be pulling the strings," suggested Stewart.

"Okay," began Lou Richards in a calm voice despite his visible excitement. "North Korea keeps announcing to the world that they're a global power. And they're constantly publicly reiterating that their global objective is to rid Asia, the Pacific, and eventually the world, of what they perceive as 'The Great American Threat'. They've always been given to hyperbole, but recently their threats have hit an all-time high, threatening the USA most recently with outright destruction.

"Even so, it seems inconceivable, given their limited economic, financial and natural resources, their social backwardness and their excessive military spending, not to mention their silence regarding the recent 'events' and 'auctions', that they're really a major player in this. Most here, I think, would agree that if North Korea *were* a major player, they'd be bragging about it all over the airwaves. No, it's much more likely, as Kate suggested, that they're playing a supportive or co-enabling role…"

"You really think so?" Kate interrupted.

"Well, I think, like you, they're probably involved in some aspects, from imagining the events to directing the auctions, and maybe, providing the field agents. These all play to their particular strengths.

"With those thoughts in mind, let's revisit these auctions a minute: My group has, for years now, been been following North Korea's burgeoning interest in cyber-warfare. Consider, for instance, the existence of their ultra-secret 'Bureau 121'. And it's certainly not news that they've been attempting to slip sleeper agents into the USA for the last twenty years. As for directing the 'auctions', they would, I assume, receive a hefty 'commission' and thereby garner the wealth they so desperately need. A single "sale" would not only provide the massive amounts of money needed to finance the rebuilding of their social infrastructure, essential to prevent an internal 'revolution-against-the-revolution', but to also fund their propaganda machine, provision their military with yet more weaponry, including nuclear weapons, and finance their secret police's efforts to continue their control of the people. All this while supporting their leaders' foibles. Don't discount their experience in cyber-warfare! North Korea may be one of the most experienced nations in regard to cyber-warfare. How many successful 'hacks' have they pulled off in the past year? One? Five? Ten?" Richards asked searching the faces around the table. "Our branch contends it's more in the neighborhood of *hundreds of thousands*, most of them successful and not reported to the public."

A sober hush spread through the room.

Chapter 26

Engines whining, the odd-shaped plane lurched forward, pressing Falk deep back into the form-fitting copilots seat of the B2 "Spirit" fighter-bomber. His hastily written orders and field notes taped against his skin beneath his flight suit already itching. The runway, barely visible through his helmet on his side of the cockpit fell quickly away and out of sight. What in a commercial airplane constantly zigzagging to avoid expanding and intersecting event echos would have taken eight to twelve hours to reach Hickam Air Base, Hawaii, would take less than four hours in the long-range military fighter-bomber, flying a path updated moment-to-moment by the Department of Defense's Advanced Hazard Warning Assistance System. Of course, no one knew how long the system would remain functional. The required computational power necessary to track and forecast the exact locations of the ever-changing intersections in relation to a fast-flying military jet increased super-exponentially each minute. At some point, even the most advanced computer systems would suffer information overload and shut down. If that happened, there would be little the pilot could do to avoid an event-echo or echo-intersection. They would simply have to slam through, lose power momentarily, and trust the plane's auto-restart functions would kick in before they crashed.

Uncomfortable in the tight, all-enclosing flight suit, Falk watched the land below melt away and flow behind him like oozing liquid butter. In the cloudless sky directly ahead, he could see a steady distant horizon, the top half a light powder blue, the bottom half a hazy mixture of greens and browns.

His first and overriding concern was whether he would arrive in Oahu early enough before the next event occurred, assuming, of course, the next event didn't show up in Anchorage, Alaska, a far less probable alternative. *Actually*, he thought, *it would be better if the next event* did *occurred there:* At the least, it would afford him additional information that might be useful to his mission in Honolulu. Better yet, the authorities there might capture an agent provocateur or her controller, making his work in Hawaii easier.

Directing his thoughts to Hawaii, he realized he would need to be at the event epicenter well before the event happened in order to observe the event process first-hand. Given his, Koski and Stewart's experiences with on-site agents, he was no longer considering trying to capture one alive. Instead he decided to direct his attention on how to try to capture and interrogate a handler or, better yet, a controller, someone who might know more about the ultimate endgame.

Falk tried to imagine himself a North Korean handler in Hawaii. He would position himself in a heavily populated area, perhaps near a university or North Korean expat community, if there was such a thing. There would likely be something like that somewhere in or near Honolulu. In time his thoughts loosened and the boredom of the flight began to take hold.

Air hissed hypnotically around the cockpit, interrupted only by occasional, hard-to-understand radio communications between the pilot and ground control. The result acted as a strong soporific, and Falk soon found himself nodding, his mind wandering from one daydream to another.

It was in just such a state that his agent's mind typically took over, and he imagined the two girls, one Oriental, the other, Caucasian or at least "American," posing as students rooming together in a nondescript house with a new, state-of-the-art outdoor satellite antenna. The Oriental girl's room would be cluttered with electronic equipment, especially this late in the event preparation process. They would be working feverishly to connect the equipment, making certain it was ready to go. Ready for what might very well prove the capstone event. The *coup de grace*. The event that would bring America to its knees.

Falk startled and shifted his weight to get a better look below, but the body straps fought against him. In the end, despite his best efforts, the harness won.

Peering out of the corner of an eye, he could see scattered, white, cotton-puff clouds projecting discrete shadows onto the surface of a vast, sparkling, deep blue ocean. Flying in the same direction as the earth's rotation made it seem forever afternoon. The feeling was one of relative peace in an otherwise crazy world.

Three hours out, his helmet crackled and the pilot's metalic voice intruded. "A colleague of yours is just off our right wingtip."

Struggling once again against the straps, twisting hard right, he saw a flash of sunlight reflect off the fuselage of a sleek-looking jet. Within it, he assumed, would be Koski, his trusted colleague and, more recently, the singular woman who had somehow found her way into his heart. Whatever lingering feelings of doubt he had about the success of his mission lifted. Raising a hand to his helmet visor, he sent her a salute, hoping she could somehow see the gesture.

"Regulations require we keep a set distance between

aircraft; however, the other pilot and I thought you and your partner might enjoy seeing each other a little bit better, at least for a moment." The distant silver jet nudged cautiously closer, until Falk could just make out its helmeted pilot and passenger. The passenger waved, and the aircraft immediately began drifting away and behind.

Ever since the first event, he and Koski had been working separately, leaving Falk feeling surprisingly awkward and incomplete. Despite his finely honed agent skills and extensive field experience, ever since he'd stepped off the plane in Laplacia, Vermont, his normally analytic mind had felt slightly off. Distracted. It was as if he were harboring an itch he couldn't locate, and for that reason, scratch. Falk made a mental note to thank the pilot for the grand gesture, and Stewart for bringing them back together on what promised to be their most challenging mission yet.

His jet abruptly lurched, sending a shiver through the plane and his tightly constrained body.

What the hell? Falk thought as the helmet earphones went dead. Glancing forward and to his left, he could see several instrument lights on the pilot's panel flashing red. It was then he realized the engines had cut off. The next moment, the floor felt like it was dropping from underneath.

What the hell? he barely had time to think a second time

before the plane rolled abruptly to the right, the nose pointing down towards a rapidly spiraling, ever expanding ocean. White caps, invisible less than a second ago suddenly appeared as pinpoint dots and a moment later took recognizable shape. The plane, he realized, was spinning downward in what airmen from the earliest days of winged flight called a "dead man's stall." It meant they were dropping like a lead weight.

Before he could think further, the plane once again shuddered, then lurched violently forward. His head filled with the scream of reawakening engines strained to their limit. *That will be the engines restarting. The pilot will be trying to break our stall*, he thought. The spinning quickly subsided, but the plane continued to accelerate nose down.

Falk felt his body press harder into his seat, as though an elephant were leaning against his chest, making it difficult to take a much needed breath. A second, more violent shudder rippled through the fuselage, as the pilot tried to pull out of the dive, causing Falk's helmet to strike the cockpit plexiglass with a loud crack, delivering a vicious blow to his left temple. Dazed, unable to focus his tearing eyes, it was all he do to filter out the nerve-wracking whine of the engines, the buzz of the multiple cockpit alarms, and contain the nausea welling up from the pit of his stomach.

His peripheral vision began to blur. He shook his head from

side-to-side, and felt a sharp pain shoot down both arms that brought more tears to his eyes. Carefully returning his head to a neutral position, he looked forward only to see dark-blue filling the entire cockpit window. He could feel the blood draining from his head, and his peripheral vision begin blackening like a closing iris. His situation was further compromised by the copious amount of sweat streaming down from his cold, clammy brow, mixing at the edges of his eyes with the tears from the pounding in his head.

Falk had barely enough time to think, *Shit! We're going to crash!* before the floor abruptly rose from underneath him and finished draining all the remaining blood from his head.

He directed a shaking hand to the outside front of his helmet in a useless attempt to brush away the copious combination of blood, sweat and tears. Unable to do so, the flow began to fill the space between his chin and the constricting neck folds of his flight suit.

"Shit, shit, shit!" he voiced, this time aloud in his helmet to himself, his voice sounding increasingly distant. Everything began to whirl and he threw up just before passing out.

A sudden chirrup pierced the air and a strong, calm, but concerned voice sounded in his ears in the now blood-sweat-and-vomit-pooled helmet. "Sorry, sir. We hit an unexpected event-echo that came at us from the side. To be honest, we're lucky the engines auto-restarted when they did. A fraction of a second later and we'd have become part of the Pacific Ocean. I was barely able to pull us out of the dive. I had to aggressively coax her nose back up without, I hope, causing you too much discomfort."

"Event-echo," Falk mumbled, then, "Discomfort," he muttered with difficulty to let the pilot know he was still alive.

"Yes, sir. The Hazard Warning System failed," the pilot continued, "just before the event-echo hit us. My instructions are to take you to your destination in the least amount of time, so we'll continue on our heading directly for Hickam Air Field." Not receiving an immediate reply, the pilot looked over at Falk and continued anxiously, "You okay, sir?"

Falk carefully stretched his neck, and not experiencing the sharp pain he'd felt earlier, flexed his fingers, arms, legs and toes to make certain he was intact and to allow the blood and vomit to pass from his helmet down into the body of his flight suit. Looking up and to his left, he could make out the near reclining silhouette of the pilot behind a reflected image of his own face in his helmet. The face staring at him looked white as chalk, except for a vivid red line running down from his left temple to his cheek. The blood was already thickening and darkening. His face felt cold and clammy, his mouth pasty and dry. He could taste the acridness of bile and the smell was…

indescribably affronting. He swallowed with difficulty. "Shit," he said, clearer, calmer and firmer than the last time.

"Sir, are you all right?" the pilot's voice crackled again in his helmet, reverberating from side to side, causing Falk's head to resume pounding.

"Yeah, well…I think so," Falk replied glad to hear his own voice sound calmly rational and not so distant. "I'm afraid, however, that I'm a horrible mess…"

"Ahhh," the crewman murmured, loosening his straps to better look over his right shoulder at his passenger. "Looks like you've a nasty cut there, sir, but the bleeding has stopped. I'll turn the oxygen up a bit. You should feel better momentarily."

Falk, hurting and still somewhat dazed, sighed. He could already hear the extra oxygen hissing into his flight helmet. "That's much better, thanks," he replied more cohesively and with as much assurance as he could muster.

"My pleasure, sir," the pilot finished, returning his attention forward and mumbling in his helmet microphone something that sounded to Falk like a distress call.

"Please make certain you're completely strapped in, sir," the pilot said. "At this speed and altitude, without Hazard Warning System support, there'll be no advanced warning should we encounter another…"

The vibration from the engines abruptly stopped, leaving

the plane slicing silently forward through the air like a thrown knife. This time instead of falling, Falk heard a single loud click followed by an explosion, and the cockpit above and the plane below him disappeared in a cloud of smoke. A moment later, still strapped to his chair, he was falling from the sky at the end of a large, orange-and-white-striped parachute. The plane's fuselage, far ahead, smashed into the ocean in a massive splash and explosion.

The next thing he knew, he was bobbing from side-to-side, the orange-and-white-striped parachute floating behind him in the water like a full skirt, creating a noticeable if temporary visual call for help.

Falk released his harness, unfastened his helmet, and bowed his filthy head to whisper a brief thanks to the God of the skies, in the same breath asking Him to protect Koski, hoping she'd survived the two event-echoes and fared better. What several hours ago had started as yet another challenging assignment was proving nothing less than a one-way ticket to hell.

Freeing himself from the constraints of the chair that had just saved his life, Falk began enumerating the pros and cons of abandoning it. Scanning the ocean about him and not seeing any sign of human life, his rattled brain began anxiously asking over and over, *Where the hell is Koski?* before he passed out.

Chapter 27

"I have to agree with Bob," said the man sitting at the far end of the Cerebrus conference table. Looking like a Sigmund Freud doppleganger, the white-bearded, middle-aged man in a dark tweed jacket raised his hand like a high school student, then, looking at his own raised hand, lowered it and shifted uncomfortably in his chair. Doctor Professor Albert Halsey, Cerebrus' Director of Political Analysis waited patiently to be acknowledged.

"Albert," Stewart called. "We'd all like to hear your take on the situation."

Halsey cleared his throat, looked anxiously at his watch then from person to person as if awaiting their individual permissions to speak, swallowed hard and began: "Despite how much effort the North Koreans put into making themselves *appear* to the world as Lou just said, we've no *proof* that they're anywhere close to having the ability to administer as complex and coordinated an operation as this. Recall the former USSR prior to *perestroika*: The Soviets' had literally hundreds of thousands of the fastest, most powerful tanks in the world, many equipped with nuclear-tipped artillery shells, all lined up several rows deep just behind the Iron Curtain. Highly visible. Attack ready. A constant reminder to NATO and the West that half of Europe could be overrun in one Blitzkrieg-like action before anyone knew it was happening.

"What they purposefully didn't share was that each tank had only five shells, one box of ammunition, and not a single replacement track link. Five shots from its cannon, a couple minutes of automatic fire exchange, and the world's foremost tanks would become little more than useless pieces of junk. Break a tread, and they would became a sitting duck, or worse, an obstacle to their own forces.

"It was the same with the Soviet Air Force at that time. It sported the fastest fighters in the world. Nothing we had could catch up with the MIG 27; hell, it could outrun our air-to-air missiles! What the Soviet propaganda machine carefully avoided disclosing, however, was was that the fighters were fuel-guzzlers. They carried only enough gas for a single 'one-way' flight in support of a major land offensive. There wasn't enough gas to return to base and refuel!"

Halsey looked at his watch, as if calculating the time he had left to speak, then continued.

"Then there was the whole facade regarding the status of their Navy, and, again, of their nuclear missile arsenal. I could go on and on.

"Despite their military *braggadocio*, it was clear to Premier Gorbachev that if the Soviet Union had to actually flex its muscle in a theater-wide conflict, they would quickly lose.

"North Korea, I believe, is in a similar situation, so to speak 'holding a propaganda tiger by the tail', pushing North Korea into taking dangerously overstated positions just like the Soviet Union did. In this case, however, North Korea isn't entirely a 'paper tiger' like we often like to think. It's more like a total destruction machine without any particular focus in regard to what it will destroy. It's simply waiting for someone—anyone—to intentionally or accidentally call them out. To me, it makes a perverse sense that they would be the organizers of the both the 'events' and 'auctions'. If successful, it would become possible for them to purchase the necessary military capacity about which they're propagandizing. Take their perspective for a moment, and I think you can easily imagine them internally justifying the risk of such a gamble in order to bring reality back in line with rhetoric. And that's my five minutes," Halsey said checking his watch and clearing his throat a second time. With that, he slumped back into his chair as if the effort of speaking had completely drained him.

"That does make sense, Albert, though I'm not certain the North Koreans have the will or the propensity to actually take on risk at that level, at least from a political perspective," the final member of the Tiger Team, Helen Schrivener, Cerebrus' Head of Liaison for Middle and Far Eastern Divisions interjected. An attractive woman in her late thirties, and considered a "heavy-weight" among Director Chiefs, she was immediately interrupted by a rejuvenated and surprisingly animated Halsey.

"From a 'political perspective'? A 'purely political perspective'?" Halsey questioned. Standing, he swept his hands to his left and right in an all-inclusive gesture, and continued. "You all must admit that the North Koreans have purpose, motive and, at least, the administrative ability. And their current situation makes them desperate enough to actually take on such risk—at least that's how I imagine their leader would view it. That they're behind it, I'm almost certain…but they could only do it with the assistance of their only close partner, China."

"Then you think China's equally involved?" Stewart asked, nodding subtly at Helen to indicate that her opportunity to speak would be neither forgotten nor lessened.

Bracing both hands on the table, Halsey explained, "Most

likely, though perhaps indirectly, *possibly* unwittingly, and always with 'plausible deniability', just in case the venture doesn't work or backfires."

"An increasingly interesting theory, but really, Albert, North Korea?" interjected Helen Scrivener. "North Korea may be an avowed enemy of the USA, and an unpredictable bastard colleague of China, but there's plenty of organizations with sufficient means and motive elsewhere throughout the world. Take the Middle East, for example: Virtually every radical faction in the Middle East is stepping up its threats against the USA in number, breadth and vehemency. These threats are sophisticated, coordinated, multi-national and have resulted in highly successful field operations. While North Korea's threats are many, and vitriolic, aside from cyber-ops, they remain mostly rhetoric and have, to the best of our knowledge, been accompanied by only a few obscure, awkward, and mostly unsuccessful field ops. Think North Korean abductions of Japanese citizens, for instance. What has that really gained them?

"The Middle East, on the other hand, is a quagmire of well-trained, well-equipped, political-religious extremists, both leaders and followers. Each faction is continuously consolidating and reconsolidating its position amongst other factions, most recently under the guise of 'radical Islam'. The result is a slowly organizing network of independent but integrated super-national criminal organizations."

Looking around the table, everyone appeared engrossed in the picture of the world Scrivener was successfully painting.

"And that's what they are in the end: organized criminal organizations," Scrivener reiterated. "Every major Middle Eastern nation—Iran, Syria, Palestine, Yemen, the list is long and growing—like China, has sufficient monetary and intellectual resources to be behind the recent events and auctions. Every Middle Eastern player has sufficient military, intelligence, criminal and often piratical resources to acquire the most advanced technology without impunity. Just look at Iran and it's 'uranium enrichment program'! Do you really think it will stop producing weapons-grade uranium because of an international *agreement*? Every Middle Eastern player has the necessary field experience to implement the events and auctions, or, at the least, participate in them.

"For decades, the American, Chinese and Russian governments as well as their attendant military-industrial complexes have been more than willing to sell sophisticated weaponry and armaments to the highest bidder, basically eliminating the need for errant organizations to fund the expensive basic research necessary to create and produce the new kinds of equipment they desire. Most weaponry advances tend to occur in small, increasingly expensive increments over a long period of time in a decidedly linear fashion. Outright purchase, on the other hand, allows the buyer to take a giant step forward. It's the same with computer technology and people's understanding of it—what the famous Russian scientist, Vladimir Vernadsky called the 'technosphere' and collectively the 'noosphere'.

"As for having physics and computer capability, Iran is long known to have it's own, covert, highly up-to-date and vastly understated but increasingly powerful physics and computational capability as a consequence of and in anticipation its ongoing 'secret' war with Israel.

"Have I missed anything? Organizational ability? Think Islamic State or Pakistan. Think ISIS—Daesh—and ask yourself if they have the determination and finances to *acquire* rather than develop the organizational, computational and military resources necessary for these events and auctions, and accomplish it all in relative secrecy. They can and do!

"Finally, while it's true that the materials and field agents associated with the 'events' belie the Chinese, it would be in the best interest of any Middle East nation to divert attention elsewhere, for example to China, while implementing a cyberwar like this one. How hard is it to label products in Chinese, and procure some Chinese or North Korean-appcaring agents and weapons? During World War II, the US and its allies successfully accomplished such a ruse on an international scale in Operation Fortitude, presenting the German's sufficiently plausible misinformation to hide the entire scope of preparations for D-Day.

"No, I think we would be amiss if we didn't seriously consider that a Middle East nation or coalition could be the organizer, implementer and seller, seeking to strengthen and extend it's global reach all the while appealing to the masses by way of its religious goal of destroying the 'Western Satan'. Behind it, indirectly, probably knowingly, but with assured 'plausible deniability' could very well be the 'new' Russia and possibly China with North Korea following."

As Scrivener sat, Jerry Falmouth rose.

"G...good points, all, Helen. I'll accede that N...North Korea and the growing Middle East C...Coalition are both capable of mounting a well-coordinated cyberwar, like our p... present situation. Our various f...field operations, during the past five years have yielded d...documents indicating that both have been actively engaged in cyberattack after cyberattack against the USA, r...reminiscent, if you will, of H...Hitler's attacks on Spain immediately preceding World War II. The Nazis used Spain as a t...testing platform for their advanced weaponry, and to test th...theater level command and control.

It was the Allies' r…reticence to r…recognize it for what it was that kept it from being acknowledged as such. The line between t…terroristic cyber-warfare and out-and-out w…war is increasingly b…blurry. Still, I imagine the current s… situation as one where either, or God f…forbid, both together in some k…kind of unholy alliance, might be t…testing their cyber weaponry and th…theater command and control capabilities."

"Both?" asked Stewart to the suddenly silent circle of experts, each pondering the implications of what had been shared. "Personally, I wish we knew more about these auctions. I feel as though we're missing something, something crucial, something vital," Stewart added, tossing the gauntlet back before the group.

"If I may, Stewart," Kate replied.

All eyes shifted to Kate Keenan.

"There's more than I was able to share in my five minutes."

Stewart surveyed the group and detecting agreement from all, replied, "Alright, the floor's yours once again," and sat.

"For the moment, let's focus on these auctions. We know the key is the use of BitCoins and BitCoin technology," she began.

"Before you go on, could you explain to those of us who are ignorant of everything 'BitCoin' exactly what it is?"

interrupted Halsey.

"Yes, of course," Kate answered. "The idea behind BitCoins is tightly linked to the increasingly sophisticated internet. A BitCoin is a digital token that can be used to make decentralized, internet-based, global transactions."

Surveying the table, Kate Keenan could see she was commanding everyone's attention.

"By 'decentralized'," she continued, "I mean there's no 'bank' involved. Furthermore, the transactions, while public, are anonymous, their anonymity coming mainly from the use of an internet-within-the-internet, the massively encrypted 'The Onion Router' network, commonly called TOR. BitCoins are issued and handled by specially dedicated TOR servers according to a fixed set of mathematical rules.

"One of them, for instance, is that the maximum number of BitCoins is fixed forever at 21 million. The system began with less than a million BitCoins in electronic circulation. One can buy existing BitCoins using any world currency from any person on the internet who has some, the 'sell price' fluctuating based on supply and demand. BitCoins back then represented 'potential currency', as there were few buyers, and a very limited number of merchants who would accept them for real goods. One could also accumulate BitCoins electronically by verifying, recording and tracking BitCoin transactions in what is called a public 'blockchain'. In this manner, participants around the world are "paid" in BitCoins for doing the accounting necessary to maintain the system. This process is called 'mining' and it's how BitCoins are 'created'."

"So the value of a BitCoin varies?" asked Halsey.

"Yes, just like stock on the stock market, except that the total number of BitCoins is permanently capped at 21 million, and the system is defined by a mathematical algorithm rather than by governments, bankers and brokers. When it started, the BitCoin was valued at one thousand three hundred and nine BitCoins to a US dollar, or about eight-hundredths of a cent."

"How long have they been around?" asked Halsey, intrigued.

"The concept was introduced on an internet discussion board in October of 2008 by a Mr. Satashi Nakamoto in a referenced 'white paper'. It was further developed and eventually implemented by a band of Nakamoto-supporters who allegedly conversed directly with Mr. Nakamoto via the internet. It wasn't until November of 2010 that the first *physical* 'exchange,' Mt.Gox, was created and the first goods transaction, supposedly two pizzas for the sum of roughly twenty-five thousand BitCoins, took place. By February 2011, there were four million BitCoins, valued roughly at parity with the US dollar, that is, one BitCoin per US dollar. That represents an enormous return for initial investment, and, remember, BitCoins were still largely unknown and unused back then.

"Several defining events helped bring BitCoins before the public: First, as a result of Wikileaks, Wikipedia lost most of it's funding. At around the same time, banks in Cyprus were failing. In each case, BitCoins retained their value and were the main currency used for securing local goods and money. Soon afterwards, there appeared a number of exchanges and internet merchants accepting BitCoins, including the notorious Silk Road. Silk Road was a market not only for domestic products, but virtually anything, legal or illegal."

"I r…remember hearing that f…federal agents shut down the S…Silk Road, but could never identify and p…prosecute the literally hundreds of criminal sellers," offered Jerry Falmouth.

"Correct," replied Kate. "While blockchains publicly list every transaction, they don't reveal the *identities* of the buyers or sellers. Since then, a second, singularly important event occurred: The 'system,' or more accurately the miners and exchanges, were hacked. Not the blockchains, however. They remained unhacked. Remember, BitCoins are like dollar bills without serial numbers. Whoever *possesses* digital BitCoins can use them as currency for any purpose anywhere in the world.

"Despite the Silk Road and numerous other 'dark' exchanges being shut down, BitCoins *continued to increase in value* to what they were just prior to these events and auctions. At that time, a BitCoin was worth roughly one thousand US dollars. The United States Financial Crimes Enforcement Center, FCEC, had independently begun investigating the 'system' wondering what was continuing to drive up BitCoin values when, in fact, its usage was foundering.

"I promised you some new and important information that might shed light on the auctions, and here it is: Ten days prior to the first event, ten million BitCoins suddenly vanished from circulation. During this time, the individual BitCoin value exploded to well over fifty thousand dollars. FCEC knew about this, but was unable to account for the anomaly, given the anonymous nature of BitCoins and the TOR net. What they *suspected* was that a person or group of persons was attempting to 'corner the market' and artificially drive up BitCoin values using some as yet undiscovered variant of the Silk Road. That, apparently, turned out to be these auctions.

"While we still haven't identified who is selling, bidding or buying, the auctions are, in fact, taking place using BitCoins on the dark TOR net. Given what we've seen so far, my group has taken to calling this new variant the 'Iron Road', and, I believe there is every indication that it is a North Korean effort."

"Why not get hold of Mr. Nakamura?" Helen Schrivener asked. "Surely he would know how to 'mine' his own creation for the information."

"Mr. Nakamura disappeared when things began to heat up, well before the events and auctions. All we really know about him is that the person, group, nation or multi-national consortium behind the creation of BitCoins exercised unparalleled cryptographic skills. As I said, no one has yet been able to break the encrypted public 'buy/sell' blockchains."

Several minutes of profound silence followed in the wake of Kate's revelation. It was Stewart who finally said, "Sounds to me like it's time for a first vote: So, who or what is behind this? North Korea? China? Russia? Organized Crime? A Middle East Consortium? Or some even more obscure, nefarious conglomeration? Albert, please pass everyone a piece of paper. Each of us will write down *one* of these choices. Kate will tally the votes—thank you, Kate—and, when she's done will read the results aloud. If there's any disagreement, we'll continue to follow Delphi protocol, that is, we'll have another discussion round and revote until we reach consensus regarding the most likely culprit on which to focus our and the nation's attention.

Chapter 28

"Tally's done," Kate Keenan announced. "We're split: North Korea with or without China's help is the 'winner' with a Middle East Coalition with or without Sino-Russian involvement a close second. Both seem plausible given what has been presented so far."

"Okay, lack of consensus during the first round is to be expected," Stewart responded. "At least we've narrowed things down to two most likely scenarios. That's where Delphi comes into play. It's time for us to assemble into two groups based on our vote. North Korea in the corner over there, the Middle East Coalition in the other corner over there. Take a few minutes to discuss the reasons why you believe your choice is true, correct or best, and be prepared to argue for five minutes for and defend it."

The participants did as instructed, taking a little less than ten minutes to reaffirm consensus within their groups and prepare.

When the ten minutes was over, David Hallard was clearly chaffing at the bit.

"What say we ask David to go first?" asked Stewart with a smile.

"Thank you. Well," began David Hallard, Cerebrus' Head of Field Operations, leaning forward and placing both hands flat on the conference table. "There's been no indication from any of our or any other agency's field agents we know of, of any increased chatter between North Korea, China, Russia and any Middle Eastern 'coalitions', criminal organizations or known terrorist groups. While our field agents have been reporting isolated instances of information sharing between dark forces, the closest thing we've come to of any major significance was the rogue action dubbed "Operation Imminent Danger" in which Cerebrus agents Koski and Falk were involved. But that was more of a localized 'terrorist' plot involving a radicalized pop star, planning to use a biological weapon to eradicate the world's assembled religious leaders last Easter at the Hollywood Bowl. His only 'outside' associate was a loosely pieced together anarchist group which he himself organized. Now, Stewart mentioned noting a North Korean linguistic pattern in our otherwise singularly uninformative 'Chinese' captive before she so inconveniently shot herself.

"The CIA has several deep agents in North Korea, who have reported that with North Korea sinking further and further into economic mire, it's assets continuing to be seized as a consequence of worldwide trading sanctions, and its efforts at 'running the blockade' being increasingly stymied, unless they do something—something drastic and soon—the nation will implode on its own and its leaders will find themselves in fear of their lives either at the hands of their own people, or facing the World Court for crimes against humanity.

"I agree with Jerry and Albert that North Korea has motive and purpose. Given the gravity of their situation, you could even call it 'need'. They're even experts at cyberwarfare. The real question then is whether they have the kind of *advanced* cyber-techology necessary to pull off the auctions, and possibly also the events.

"Many envision North Korea as an uneducated, backwards country of obligate followers. While much of its *population* fits this picture, its chosen few are quite the opposite: Their techno-elite are highly educated youth, tasked specifically with thinking 'out of the box'." David Hallard straightened, lifted his hands from the table and conceded the floor to the next in his group, Kate Keenan.

Kate and Stewart had been whispering together while David spoke. Breaking from each other, Kate Keenan,

Cerebrus' Chief Technical Advisor, stood, looked Stewart in the eyes, and, after receiving an affirmative nod, began. "What I'm about to share with you comes from a sensitive project I've been working within Cerebrus.

"In the late 1990's, we became aware that the North Korean military, frustrated with competing in the world of big-time conventional and NBC—Nuclear-Biological-Chemical— warfare, committed ten, later twenty, and currently as much as thirty percent of their budget to cyber-warfare. This was an arena in which they *could* compete. Beefing up their universities, the military began recruiting the best of their best computer graduates to a secret 'bureau' called simply by the numeric acronym, 'twenty-one', later, 'one-twenty-one'. Headquartered in in the Moonshin-dong area of Pyongyang, the bureau quickly outgrew the limited internet access available from within North Korea.

"In 2005, we traced their activities to Shenyang in China's nearby Liaoning Province. Operating under the guise of a 'North Korean Cultural Unit', the 'hacker hut', as the basement of the North Korean tourist hotel and restaurant came to be called, began testing their cyber-warfare skills using China's more open access to the internet. China continues to deny that it is in collusion with what now became called 'Bureau 121' and that the bureau even exists; however, our agents have documented North Korean and Chinese officials, including key high-ranking military figures, frequenting the restaurant and subsequently the 'basement'.

"By 2009, Bureau 121 had grown from twenty hackers to over five thousand 'specialists', responsible, we believe, for a growing number of aggressive cyber-attacks against South Korea and later the USA and EU. It's my opinion that their level of coordination, sophistication, and more importantly, success at penetrating US cyber-defenses, make them quite capable of instigating and supporting, with China's help, much of what we're seeing now." Kate paused, waiting for Stewart to confirm permission to continue.

He did.

"In 2010, the United States' National Security Agency— NSA—our more public sister organization, tasked Cerebrus with 'back-hacking' into North Korea's computer network. It took some time, but we were eventually able to secretly insert some specially-constructed Sysnet-like code similar to what was used to obfuscate Iran's uranium enrichment efforts. The code has allowed us to track Bureau 121's cyber operations. NSA has used and continues to use this 'trap door' in the Bamboo Curtain to United States' advantage.

"Having access to their computer systems, and knowing their particular 'fingerprint', we have been able to attribute various hacking efforts to them or not. Gentlemen and ladies, I can now state without reservation that the auction internet code has 'North Korea' written all over it. Of course, it's impossible to prove, given their careful use of the super-encrypted TOR internet.

"The catch to all this is that however coordinated and sophisticated North Korea's Bureau 121's attacks have become, they've never crossed the line from cyber-hacking to what we seem to be experiencing with these events and auctions. I don't believe they have the resources to move from hacking to tactical military cyber-intrusion. However, North Korea could have easily *obtained* it by secret agreement from its big brother and only technologically-significant benefactor, China. In return, the situation would allow the Chinese to use the North Koreans to field test new weapons of war including cyberwar, while at the same time maintaining plausible deniability."

"I have to agree with Kate," Albert Halsey, Director of Political Analysis and a strong member of the 'North Korea' scenario group stated. "North Korea is at the least the mostly likely instigator. Up to now, China, succumbing to global political pressures, has always jerked North Korea's leash whenever it stepped out of line, so in this instance, I suspect the Chinese didn't know the extent to which North Korea was applying this technology, purchased, shared, transferred or stolen, against the USA.

"I'd like to present an alternative scenario: What if North Korea, through these efforts, saw the opportunity of maneuvering it's leash-master, China, and United States into a centerstage confrontation? North Korea could stand on the sidelines and watch the two duke it out, waiting until both nations were too engaged to stop and redirect any final efforts at North Korea, before directing their own final effort at their stated enemy, the USA. North Korea could end up the 'savior' of China, or the uncontested victor against both nations. A very clever scenario, you must agree. Were it true."

"F...Furthermore," Jerry Falmouth, Chief of Information Analysis, added while staring at a scowling Helen Schrivener, Cerebrus' vocal Far Eastern Liaison, "N...North Korea is well p...positioned in the worldwide terrorist network to accomplish just such a f...feat. Agreed, five years ago, that title would have been reserved for acknowledged t...terrorist organizations throughout the M...Middle East. But these d...days, that label has expanded to include r...rogue nations and even organized c...criminal organizations perpetrating multi-national crime as a 'b...business'. Add to these the more nefarious multi-national c...corporations, which have no allegiance to any nation or creed other than p...profit. 'If it makes m...money or increases power, it's right,' seems to be their new ethic, w...whether that means working temporarily with extreme r...religious, nationalistic, c...criminal or other corporate organizations. Up to now, these 'soft t...terrorists' have operated pretty much independent of each other, but what if N...North Korea proposed an economic venture in everyone's s...shared best interest? Wh...what if that's what these auctions are about?" Scanning the faces at the table, Falmouth watched many nod in agreement.

Chapter 29

Koski waited patiently in the driver's seat of her damaged, rented car, watching a small single-prop-engine Cessna float down from the sky, wings fluttering, its nose pointed slightly to the side to compensate for a slightly oblique headwind. It was barely ten minutes since Stewart had called her and ordered her to the Fulton airport to await transportation to, of all places, Honolulu, Hawaii. Visiting the fiftieth state had always been a dream of hers, her work never before taking her to "paradise." It was a dream she had been saving to share with Falk, now that their relationship had advanced from collegial to romantic. She had never imagined when first assigned as an interagency videographer on Operation Who's Killing All the Lawyers that her association with the irascible man would progress to this. Actually, "could" would be more truthful than "would" as they both carried so much baggage from their earlier lives.

Their work together on The Judas List caper brought them

closer, but it was during the multiple life-threatening incidents in Operation Imminent Danger that they discovered each harbored more concern for the other than him- or herself. That particular "aha" moment opened a deeply hidden, mutual desire. Since then their relationship had taken on a life of its own, progressing at every opportunity. If there was such a thing as destiny or fate, then it was strongly insinuating itself into her life. A long neglected part of her heart was still finding it difficult to believe in this second chance, while the rest pushed her relentlessly forward.

This was the first time since they'd begun working together that they'd had to split up. Now, if only that same destiny or fate that brought them together would just…

Koski startled at what sounded like a loud, distant rumble of thunder, noticing the next instant what appeared to be a fighter jet appear from within a bank of clouds, scream down to a point just above the end of the short runway to hover in mid-air. Moving sideways like a metallic crab, the plane slowly finished descending, stopping on the tarmac close to the control tower next to where she was parked. It took a moment for her to realize that this awkward monstrosity was the "military transport" which Stewart had arranged. A good thing, too, as, given a choice, she would have balked and declined. As it was, she was quite simply too surprised to object.

The plane's whining engines shut down and the cockpit cover slid back, revealing a pilot encased in a flight suit and white helmet. The man, assuming it was a man, immediately began waving and pointing, indicating she was to take the navigator/passenger seat behind him. Stunned, Koski gathered together the papers scattered across the passenger seat of her car, unshouldered her weapon, and removed the chamber round and clip, stuffing it all roughly into the standard Cerebrus-issue brown leather briefcase she had with her. Taking a deep breath, she returned her attention to the waiting pilot and plane.

The pilot, still in the front seat, was waving her towards the plane, if anything more ardently than at first. Tossing the keys onto the driver's seat, she exited the car and began jogging towards the plane. It was at this point the pilot climbed out of the cockpit and onto the back of the wing. Taking off his helmet, he knelt and extended a hand in greeting towards her. Stopping just before the back of the wing, she offered her hand to him in return greeting.

Grasping her hand, he pulled her up onto the yellow-outlined area of the fuselage where he was standing. The area was small, forcing them uncomfortably face-to-face.

"Flight Lieutenant Roger Styles at your service, ma'am," the tall, young man offered, attempting a salute while trying not to touch his passenger. Given the limited space, the salute ended up a feeble and embarrassing one.

Immediately reaching back into the cockpit, he pulled out a bulky flight suit, boots and helmet like his own. "I need you to slip into these as quickly as possible, ma'am." Glancing at his watch, he continued, businesslike, "We need to leave in less than three minutes in order to avoid the next echo-intersection."

Koski scanned the man from his midnight black hair, bright grey eyes, square clean-shaven chin and lean physique to his standard-issue flight boots. Taking the flight suit and boots in hand, she answered, "Koski. Cerberus field agent. And where exactly am I to accomplish a less-than-three-minute change of clothes, captain? It is, captain, is it not?"

"Lieutenant, ma'am. Flight Lieutenant Roger…"

"Where am I to change, lieutenant?" Koski asked again, raising her briefcase. "There's a weapon inside with the clip and chamber round removed," adding as she stared at the tiny back seat, "and I'm claustrophobic."

Lieutenant Styles nodded his understanding. "Thank you for telling me, ma'am. I suggest you change under the wing. Place your clothes in the briefcase, and, I'm sorry, but you've now less than two minutes."

With the lieutenant's assistance, Koski climbed off the wing, changed clothes and packed her 'civies' into the briefcase as fast as humanly possible. As she climbed awkwardly back onto the wing, the lieutenant checked his watch and pointed to the second seat. "If you don't mind, ma'am, we need to leave. Now. Please take your seat. I'll attach the helmet and strap you in. We've only moments to spare."

As soon as she was strapped into the narrow passenger seat, her pilot slipped the briefcase inside the cockpit alongside her seat and, talking calmly, placed the solid-white helmet, which had no way she could see to look out, over her head and locked it in place. Her flight suit instantly began hissing and adjusting to her figure. Ten seconds later, the plane shuddered, lurched, and Koski felt the fighter rise vertically. Looking out of the helmet's surprisingly translucent faceplate, her claustrophobia abated as she turned her head from side to side to watch the ground disappear. After rising about fifty feet, the plane hovered, rotated one hundred eighty degrees and abruptly thundered off into the same clouds from which it had appeared.

As the engines settled to a low constant growl, a rich masculine voice sounded in her helmet coming from every direction: "Welcome aboard, Agent Koski. I will be your pilot and flight crew for your trip to Honolulu, Hawaii, where it is currently a balmy 78 degrees. You're flying in the newest modification of a Marine Corps Vertical Short Take-Off and Landing F35B, nicknamed "Lightning III," the most prominent modifications being two seats instead of one and an extended fuel capacity. I noticed your concern when I locked on what appeared to be an opaque flight helmet, which you can see is anything but."

Koski took in the surprisingly wide view afforded by the unusual helmet, nodding to no one in particular, listening carefully while Lieutenant Styles droned on about the wonders of the cramped 'VSTOL' jet. In the end, what should have been a less than four-hour fighter jet flight to Honolulu ended up taking all of six plus hours due to a mid-air refueling, and a number of sudden, last moment zigzags to avoid event-echoes and echo intersections working their way westward.

Sitting in the cramped cabin, encased in the strange, continuously self-adjusting flight suit, she looked forward over the pilot's shoulder at the horizon and settled in for the flight. Eventually, the never-darkening corn-blue sky above abruptly extended below the plane to indicate they had began their flight over open ocean.

Traveling west, the day remained a forever afternoon, and the combination of the bright sun, the constant growl of the engines, the dull hiss of the aircraft slipping through the air, and the occasional chatter of the pilot to various ground controllers as they passed from one control area to the next, conspired to make her drift off to sleep, dreaming of warm sand and swaying palm trees.

A loud crackle, and the pilot's intrusive voice yanked her out of her slumber. "Ma'am, there's a colleague of yours just forward of the left wingtip."

Squirming in her seat to see, she could just make out an all-black, wedge-shaped triangle, and a helmeted passenger saluting at her. Knowing that she and Falk were at last back together made her blush. Thankfully, wrapped in her flight suit and helmet, flying in a military airplane at an unimaginable speed in the sparse upper atmosphere, no one would ever notice.

Her plane drifted nearer his and she returned his salute with a wave. After their brief reunion, Falk's aircraft drifted away and ahead. Whatever awaited them at their destination, Koski felt a wave of gratitude that they would at least be facing it together.

Just as she was ready to resettle in, her jet lurched, the engines stopped, and she felt blood rush to her upper body and flood her face, as if she were blushing again, but this time more extremely and without reason. The plane abruptly shook as the engines auto-restarted and she felt her body pressed hard into her seat. Any panic attacks were overridden as she watched, wide-eyed, Falk's plane begin spiraling nose down towards the ocean below. A moment later, the headphones inside her helmet crackled with chatter between her pilot and Falks', and her plane began a controlled nose dive, following Falk's plane but slower and from a distance.

The hazy corn-blue that had surrounded the plane was suddenly replaced by a blanket of endless, tiny, white dots against a dark blue background. Koski's mind shouted, *Waves! Whitecaps!* in frightened recognition, as Falks' plane shuddered and discharging a belch of flame and smoke, it's engines at last reigniting.

Falk's jet immediately leveled and began shakily climbing, while her plane shot upwards, as if to garner a better view. She felt her stomach sink and saw sparkles appear and dance before her eyes. The next moment, her flight suit hissed and tightened about her lower body, and the sinking feeling in her stomach stopped and the delicate sparkles returned to wherever it was they had previously been. Her jet resumed smooth and level flight, some distance above and behind Falk's.

Koski's helmet suddenly filled with Lieutenant Style's calm voice: "Sorry ma'am. We hit an unexpected event-echo, and, while our plane responded admirably, your friend's encountered some significant problems. They *almost…*"

Before he could finish, Koski's earphones died, and she felt herself tossed forward into her restraining straps, her helmet whipping forward, barely missing the back of the Lieutenant's seat. It seemed like Style, for some reason, had suddenly cut all power to the engines, and the plane had stopped in midair. The next moment the nose pointed down, where, over the pilot's shoulder, ahead and below, she saw two brilliant flashes, and watched in slow motion, two seats eject from the black moth of a plane that tumbled into ocean in an huge spray immediately engulfed in an explosion of flame, smoke, and pieces. One moment the flash was visible, the next, her own aircraft's engines had restarted, her pilot had regained control and her plane had streaked past. It all happened so fast, Koski didn't have time to see if Falk or the pilot had landed safely in the water below.

The plane slowed and made a sharp turn. Lieutenant Style's calm voice immediately cut in: "Sorry, ma'am. Our companion plane is down. I'm circling to try to locate survivors." There was something in his tone when he said "try to locate survivors" that sent a chill down her spine.

Completing a full circle, the VSTOL came to a helicopter-like pause above and to the side of the area where the plane had hit the ocean. At Lieutenant Style's command, they began a search of the area, the pilot concentrating on left side, Koski the right.

There was no sign of wreckage, ejection seats or parachutes. Nothing. Nothing at all but endless choppy, white-capped waves. From where they hovered, the ocean looked like a huge blanket of ominous black dappled by small white polka dots.

"It's not unusual not to find anything on first glance, ma'am," the pilot assured her, turning the plane in a slow 360-degree circle, but his assurance did little to quiet her heart. *It's when you think you've lost someone that you learn how much they really mean to you*, she thought, her heart feeling as if it were tearing apart. She realized in that moment how much she had come to love the incorrigible man always ready to put his life on the line for her and his country.

"We're running low on fuel, ma'am, and, given the collapse of the ground-based Hazard Warning Assistance System, our own situation is highly volatile. From here on, we'll be flying by the seat of our pants, meaning we will have no more advance warning regarding echo-intersections. I've radioed the impact area coordinates to Honolulu area military air traffic control as well as input a report into our in-flight recorder. I've also issued a general SOS in addition to your colleague's Mayday. I would like to to stay and search a few more minutes, but we need to continue on our flight plan in order to get you to Honolulu before fuel runs out."

Koski felt sick. Was this how her "second chance" at a relationship was to end? Before it even had the opportunity to formally begin? Shaking her head to clear her mind, she asked the pilot to do one more sweep, a little lower this time. Just one more, she begged, until the lieutenant reluctantly complied. Taking the plane lower was risky. It could be easily flipped by an errant updraft, and would be unable to recover if another intersection hit them.

It was in the last quarter of this second sweep that Koski spotted an ejection seat bobbing up and down with what looked to her like a rapidly sinking orange and white tail. "There!" she shouted, trying inanely to point and, realizing the impracticality of her action in the tight cockpit quarters, added, "To your right. Low. About two o'clock."

"I see it, ma'am!" Style answered, nudging the plane forward while banking to get a better view and hopefully identify the occupant.

"I can't tell..." Koski began to say, when the water about the seat changed in color from inky blue to white and began to boil.

"What the...?" the pilot began, as the water lightened and frothed in a long, wide, whale-like swath, the ejection seat directly forward of it's middle. Seconds later, the top of a submarine sail parted the surface.

Lieutenant Style began backing the VSTOL away, even as he broadcast, "Yankee-alpha-romeo-three-six-niner reporting the surfacing of a submarine…" followed, when the the full sail was in view and it's cyrillic marks accompanied by a set of numbers and a large red star became apparent, "…of a Russian Yassen-class submarine…" The deck hatch opened below them and several armed Russian sailors ran to the ejection seat now fully separated from its parachute and resting next on the submarine's deck.

"Identifying marks, kilo-three-niner-two 'Severodvinsk'. Submarine is attempting recovery of one of the ejected crew from our downed companion…"

Koski watched the Russian sailors lift a limp flight-suited body from the ejection seat and carry the body on their shoulders to the open hatch.

"Falk?" she whispered, unable to make out the captured man's identity as it slipped down the hatch.

"Joe?" she asked again, as if by asking again and using his first name, she could somehow assure that it *was* him and that he was still alive.

The hatch closed and the submarine immediately began descending back into the swirling waters.

In the aircraft, a buzzer sounded. "Ma'am, we need to get the hell out of here. That submarine is state-of-the-art and has the ability to take us down anytime their captain wants.

"Our navy already has this location from the Mayday and

SOS, and I've conveyed the name of the specific submarine. America and Russia will most likely soon be working on what to do about their captive, but like I said, we've got to get out of here."

Before the lieutenant had finished his monologue, the plane was pointing 180 degrees away from where the incident had taken place, its engines screaming, its fuselage straining to get as far away from the submarine as possible.

Chapter 30

"It's time for someone to play Devil's advocate," answered Helen Schrivener. "Does anyone at this table really think North Korea capable of leading a multifarious, dark, international consortium? One of *global* extent? Does anyone here other than Kate, David, Jerry and our leader *really* believe North Korea cares one whit about what's going on in the 'outside' world other than to take propaganda advantage of world events for its own purposes?"

Kate, hearing Helen Schrivener's challenge, hesitated, looking to Stewart for permission to speak. Stewart surveyed the room, paused, checked his watch, then nodded his approval for her to speak yet again.

"First," Kate Keenan stated, "my section has narrowed down the location of the likely auctioneer to an area in the Far Eastern portion of Asia where Russia, China and North Korea all converge. Unfortunately the exact location, which might give us more information on the actual perpetrator, hasn't yet been resolved.

"But given this information, while Bureau 121's hackers have been stepping up the number and scope of their cyber-attacks, we've noticed a new and very disconcerting trend in BitCoin usage.

"As I mentioned earlier, it was discovery of The Silk Road that prompted us to reconsider its possible tactical and strategic uses. People were selling not just merchandise, but also drugs, human slaves, and exotic and illegal armaments like former USSR tanks, missiles, uranium, even weapons of mass destruction. From there it would be a small step to selling 'contracts' to remove individuals for control of oil, water, food, cities, regions, even nations. What better way to broker and 'consolidate' wealth and power until the Silk Road was shut down? And remember: there can never be more than 21 million BitCoins in circulation. That means as the number approaches this limit, the relative value of any one BitCoin will vastly increase, and, from everything my section has seen, that's exactly what's happening.

"By participating in the BitCoin world, my section has been able to document an extraordinary increase in BitCoin values during the past four events to a current value of *several million dollars US per BitCoin*. This goes way beyond supply and demand. What it means is that BitCoins are likely being used and manipulated in these auctions to launder money. BitCoins, given their anonymous nature, are perfect for that.

"In the last three weeks we watched twelve million BitCoins disappear from circulation and then suddenly re appear. At this moment, the current exchange value is *twenty million dollars US per BitCoin*. That provides a laundering capacity of four hundred trillion dollars worth of currency, and the bidding war has yet to reach it's peak. Given the trend, by the time of the next event all twenty-one million BitCoins will likely be in circulation at an estimated value of *five-hundred to a thousand-million dollars US per BitCoin*, for a total laundering and purchasing capacity of roughly *twenty-one quadrillion dollars*. One can only imagine the auctioneer's fee."

Kate's disclosure animated Jerry Falmouth, who accepted the right to speak from Kate and Helen and immediately launched into his own passionate argument. "F…Freed from financial and economic constraints, N…North Korea would be able to pursue its stated primary interests without c… constraint. And how could they b…best accomplish this? One assumes that, simply by hosting the auctions, th…they would amass financial resources well beyond that of any other n… nation, including their stated arch enemy, the USA. N…North Korea has watched Ch…China attempt to accomplish the defeat of the USA by temporarily letting go of 't...true' Communism and substituting profit-motive c...capitalism, but, of course, its leaders can't publicly acknowledge that, not without losing d...dictatorial control over their g... government.

"That m...means to me that N...North Korea has to be the s...seller, at least until it has accumulated enough f...fees from brokering to allow *it* to p...play in the 'big sandbox', too. Given what I've h...heard so far, it will reach that p...point just in time for the auctioning off of Hawaii and, one assumes, the W...West Coast and Pacific Trust Islands. And, we all have to acknowledge the p...possibility, that this next auction might actually include Pacific Rim *countries* as well. That could include Indonesia, Australia, and J...Japan, territories N... North Korea has at one time or another greatly c...coveted. And should N...North Korea's ambitions increase in p... proportion to its increasing w...wealth and p...power, the next auction or subsequent auctions might also include Eastern R... Russia, Alaska, Western Canada, Central America, C...Coastal South America, even Ch...China.

"Initially, North Korea needed sufficient b...buyers, either competing or working in c...concert, to amass the immense initial monetary assets it n...needed simply to survive. That requires dark money. Lots and lots of laundered d...dark money. And since the initial auctions have th...thus far been strictly for United States p...property, the participants would likely be ones that, for one reason or another, harbor a gr... grudge against the USA or its allies. Maybe even a gr...grudge against *all* the n...nations of the world that have participated in any way in restraining N...North Korea. Or their focus may instead b...be against 'United States Imperialism', d... democracy or c...capitalism. Such an idea isn't n...new. But it would represent a d...dangerous, re-envisioning of a *new* New W...World Order like so many talk of and fear these d...days." With that, Jerry Falmouth sighed and fell back into his chair.

Stewart noted the eyes of everyone sitting around the table wide with concern. Slowly attention turned to a tense looking Franklin Gaston, Cerebrus' Programs Manager. Frank was sitting in the midst of the Middle East Coalition group with Helen Schrivener, who was visibly encouraging him to speak.

"Whether or not that's truly valid," Gaston began, "remains to be seen. I must admit, however, based on what I've just heard, it seems that North Korea by itself *would* be capable, through subterfuge and with a bit of assistance, of devising, organizing and implementing the kind of attack we're experiencing. While I still advocate a Middle Eastern Consortium, here's an afterthought on the North Korean scenario: The bidders won't likely fear that North Korea will cheat them and try to 'take over the world', not with the successful buyers possessing in hand what they consider to be agreements of regional purchase or control. That, of course, assumes that America's ability to mount a cohesive defense ultimately collapses, as it appears to be doing right now. Actually, I am suddenly reminded that during the last decade, the USA experienced near *financial* collapse *several* times. These events and auctions, however, represent something else. I think of it as a tipping point. If North Korea's truly behind them, then it should, even now, be near rich enough to break entirely free of sanctions and achieve it's wildest dreams, cementing in its current regime while at the same time eliminating its perceived worst enemy."

"Anyone have more to add?" Stewart asked as soon as Gaston had finished.

The tense silence suggested not, but before Stewart could call for a second round of voting, a muted alert sounded and a red colored dot appeared in the center of the situation screen behind him immediately next to where Spokane, Washington, was located. Everyone's cell phones began ringing. Stewart turned his face away from the table and the myriad conversations that were taking place to take a call from Colonel Rellin.

"Well, Stewart, it is exactly as we feared," Rellin confimed, "but with a small yet significant twist: This time the event epicenter is located in the center of urban Spokane, and the echo-waves are disrupting things on a much bigger scale than before. Looks like your idea that the three previous events were preludes to something bigger and more aggressive were true after all.

"Reports are coming in of cars, buses, trains and airplanes, all momentarily stalling wherever an event-echo passes over them. Worse, echoes from the other events have already begun reaching Eastern Washington, and will soon begin intersecting with those from this new event. The situation is already heavily stressing the Western power grid. Train stations, airports, hospitals, radio and television stations, military bases, the national guard, everything, after going out, is being switched to emergency power, or, where there is no emergency power available, they're simply working as best they can. Our NSA analysts project an imminent general blackout in the Northwest that will spread across the United States, taking down every regional power grid in its path. This one is lethal. And it should hit Seattle, its port and the nearby Naval, Air and Army facilities very soon."

"Was there an auction?" asked Stewart.

"Yes. Same as the other events, but this time, we had all available military and governmental resources poised and ready to watch, observe and analyze. We may not yet know how to stop it, but we're getting pretty darn close to being able to predict where the next event and auction will occur and what it's effects will be. Everything points to the next epicenter being in urban Honolulu, Hawaii.

"Although we still don't know the identities of the bidders, the ultimate buyer or the seller, this time we were more successful tracking the flow of BitCoins through the dark TOR system. I can now say with reasonable assurance that this auction was the biggest yet, it's total value close to three hundred *trillion* U.S. dollars, depending on when and how the BitCoins exchanged were actually purchased, and how the base currency, whatever it was, was laundered. In today's market, we're estimating the seller's commission at roughly *one hundred trillion U.S. dollars…*"

"God almighty! That's…" began Stewart.

"Yeah," replied Rellin. "Multiply that by the number of auctions so far and it's going to be more than the USA's gross national product and debt combined. Looks like we're approaching the endgame, and it looks like it's going to happen in Honolulu."

"I've just sent Koski and Falk there…" Stewart replied, the tone of his voice betraying equal amounts of satisfaction, determination and concern.

Chapter 31

Stewart removed his cellular from his ear and held it at his side, his hand hanging limply. Turning back to the assembled group, he said with finality, "We must complete this exercise."

"I've one more thing to add," interrupted Kate. "It occurs to me that, in spite of the insights we've gained and our closeness to consensus, we've still not come up with a way to stop the events and auctions from happening. We're closer than ever to a possible *why*—and attendant who, what, when and where—but we're just as helpless now as we were before at stopping the nation's fall into chaos. We may have ferreted out the purpose, and even the most probable instigator, but we still don't know *how* the *events* are propagated."

Everyone quieted and took a seat around the table while Kate assumed a command position next to the situation screen. Pointing with a finger at Laplacia, Vermont, and tapping the monitor screen at each subsequent event epicenter, she said, "I initially envisioned what we're seeing as a row of falling dominoes, ending in the collapse of our government, but now I'm wondering, given the change from country to urban epicenter, if the present event might represent the first in a *new* line of dominoes.

"With whatever we can glean from Spokane, and with Koski and Falk in place in Hawaii well before the next event, we might, this time, be able to capture the agents, their handlers or controllers for questioning. Given what Mr. Stewart shared regarding the nature of the Oriental agent he attempted to interrogate, I say let Koski and Falk do what they're best at doing: dealing with the agents, handlers and controllers. In short, I now believe it really doesn't matter so much what we come to consensus about at this moment, but more that we're finally able to *focus our efforts* in the most productive direction. What we need is another field team working alongside Koski and Falk to identify the *how* and possibly prevent the next event in Hawaii from happening. What we really need is…"

"You, Kate," completed Stewart for those sitting anxiously around the table. "We need *you*, working the technological aspect *in the field*, focused entirely on *how* the events are propagated and might be stopped, in parallel with Koski and Falk."

Stewart returned his cellphone to his ear, and issued the beleaguered Colonel Rellin yet another priority request for air transportation, this time for Kate Keenan to join Koski and Falk in Hawaii as soon as possible. This time, however, Colonel Rellin balked, military planes being subject to rapidly increasing priorities, acknowledging that he would make the arrangements if Stewart would provide a Cerebrus plane. Steward reluctantly agreed.

Pocketing his phone, he nodded to Kate to acknowledge that preparations were underway, then, he made a sweeping gesture that encompassed everyone sitting about the table. "I agree with everything Kate's just said. It's absolutely clear to me that we need her in the field more than we do here. But I still think a true consensus opinion from this group will be useful to the Joint Chiefs as well as our three agents. So, I reiterate: It's time for a second vote. Let's finish this Delphi session and arm our nation and field agents with the best intelligence advice possible at this time. Any objections?'"

Everyone around the table looked to their left and right, and seeing no dissenters, retook up paper pen and scribbled a vote. Moments later, Kate, having collected the sheets and counted them, announced simply, "North Korea. Unanimous."

As each member rose and prepared to leave the room to apply what they had as a group decided to his or her particular area of expertise, Kate slid to Stewart's side. "You know, Tom, except for Operation Finding Kate after which you recruited me, I've never actually 'been in the field'. I've always been..."

The phone in Stewart's hand buzzed.

"Stewart here," he announced, signaling for everyone to remain in place for the moment while turning his face aside. "Yes. Yes." The moment he signed off, the phone buzzed again. "Stewart here. Yes. No. Yes. I'm sending Kate."

Closing his cell phone, Stewart turned to address his audience. "The first call was about Falk. He was in a stealth B2 bomber-jet about two hundred miles out of Oahu when the plane's engines shut down..."

The collective intake of breath could be heard throughout the room.

"The second was about Koski. She was in a military fighter immediately behind Falk. They experienced a similar shutdown, but their engines restarted in time. They had just enough fuel to follow Falk's plane down, mark it's position, and continue on to Hickam Airfield on Oahu."

Fixing his eyes on Kate, Stewart continued: "I've informed Koski you're coming. Looks like our Honolulu field operation's going to depend entirely on you and her."

"Yes, sir," answered Kate seriously, turning and walking towards the door. Stopping just before exiting, she turned to face the group, offer a jaunty military-like salute and a decisive, "Yes, Sirs!" before leaving.

One by one, the members of the Tiger Team left the room. When at last it was empty, Stewart slumped into a chair to steal a moment and think.

A North Korean venture made sense.

He imagined the various dark elements of the world negotiating, forming and reforming alliances in preparation for each auction, each alliance intent on winning the next bid and "rights" to a region of what was rapidly becoming the "former USA." Would these players come together in the end? Who would eventually "own" the former United States of America? What would the consequences be? Would there be anyone left to jump in and protect the world from destroying itself as the world's policeman, the "good ol' USA", had done so many times in the past? If the criminal element took precedence, it would likely result in organized crime at a level never before imagined. And until the "new" New World Order, or whatever it finally called itself came into being, what would happen to the balance of power that had served to protect the world and humanity from utter destruction?

The world would, he decided, most likely be engulfed in a power struggle of epic proportions that would bring out and sadly legitimize the worst of anarchy, crime, militarism, capitalism, and, if, as the Tiger Team suspected, North Korean despotism. At the least, the newly purchased, "autonomous regions" of the former USA could be expected to immediately begin negotiating between each other to form new political, economic or ideological consortiums. The number of permutations were as staggering as Stewart's wildest imaginings, and, unfortunately, none bode well.

Chapter 32

Kate's transport arrangements happened so fast she barely had time to exit the building before she was met in front of Cerebrus' headquarters by a sleek, black government limousine. A "man in black" escorted her into the car. Once inside, Kate chose the front-facing couch seat at the back. "No point in getting too comfortable, ma'am. We'll be arriving at the airport very soon," the man said, driving skillfully into traffic. Having said what was apparently required, the man returned his attention to driving, providing Kate a short, but welcome modicum of privacy.

Relaxing on the smooth leather, she did a quick inventory of her travel resources. She hadn't had time to pack clothes or even piece together a travel bag. All she had was what she wore to work that day and whatever makeup she had in her purse.

She was interrupted in her task by the driver.

"This is for you, ma'am, compliments of Mr. Stewart," her driver said, holding a shoulder bag at length towards her without turning around. Kate scuttled forward, grasped it from the man's hands and returned to her seat. Opening it, she was delighted to see a variety of amenities including a pack of washlets, a fold-out hair brush, several sandwiches, a bottle of water and a blow-up neck pillow.

Before she could sort through the remainder of the much-appreciated provisions, the limousine slowed and passed through a gate into a nondescript private airfield where a single sleek, white commercial jet with upturned wingtips and a pregnant bump slightly amidships lay poised and ready, engines whining. The limousine proceeded to the foot of the passenger ramp and stopped.

"Your plane, ma'am," the man who had handed her the flight bag said, opening the car door for her.

The plane was impressive. It bore no commercial markings, only the minimum required identification numbers. Noting its eight passenger windows, Kate wondered with whom she would be flying. Climbing up the ramp, she was greeted by a uniformed flight attendant, who ushered her into the main cabin.

The interior was decorated in calm, pastel earth tones. The attendant offered her seating in one of two, facing, plush leather, executive-style chairs, one in front, the other behind a sizable work table. On the other side of the plane was a long leather sofa, extending the length of the interior. Sitting in the further executive chair, the flight attendant buckled her in, walked silently forward and closed the pressure hatch. Scanning the interior disbelievingly, Kate became aware that she would be the only passenger aboard this flight.

As the plane rolled down the runway, the flight attendant returned to advise Kate of the safety features of the Gulfstream G650ER, which blessedly included a shower and a closet full of clothes, all in exactly her size chosen by fashion-conscious preflight attendants on contract to Cerebrus. *They've gone all out for me,* she thought. *Or, this is all that happened to be left at the time,* her unconscious mind mulled, adding, *or this is an elegant goodbye for a mission from which I am not likely to return.* Her first thought was her first choice, she told herself. Irrespective of the situation awaiting her at the other end, this portended to be a most pleasant flight, and she would at least arrive fresh and well dressed.

Chapter 33

The two o'clock Hawaiian sun pressed heavily on the red-haired CIA officer's exposed lily-white face and arms. The burning sunlight was made even hotter and more intense by his standing, unshaded and restless, on the hot black asphalt tarmac at Hickham Air Force Base, located not far from Pearl Harbor Naval Base. Agent Ben Azaga, a fit, clean-shaven man in his early 40s, wearing an aloha shirt opened at the neck, white linen pants and a white linen tropical jacket with the sleeves rolled up, raised a bare forearm to wipe off the sweat that was beading on his forehead. New beads immediately replaced them, coalescing and flowing in small rivulets down his face. *Sweat is supposed to make you feel cooler not hotter*, he thought.

He'd never experienced anything like this in his natal Ireland or on the Continent where he'd recently been loaned by British MI5 to the US CIA. *Only the American CIA*, he mused, *would have the gall to transfer a man with such fair skin, acclimatized to cold, clouds and rain, to a location with such intensely unremitting sunlight.*

Azaga shrugged to readjust the uncomfortable shoulder holster sticking like strapping tape against his thoroughly soaked chest. A gentle, flower-scented breeze mercifully rustled his red, wavy hair, providing a moment of relief. But only a moment. It was one of those days in paradise when the trade-winds were absent, replaced by a southeast "Kona" wind blowing off of Kilauea volcano on Big Island. The effect was like that of standing in front of a giant hot hair dryer. Kona winds further portended heavy evening humidity and unremittingly uncomfortable nights.

Where the hell is the military plane carrying that hot-shot Cerebrus agent whom I'm supposed to meet? he thought looking at his wrist watch for the umpteenth time over the last hour. True, they supposedly had another twenty-four hours before the next predicted "event," hopefully the final one, unfortunately, the one that was predicted to be the last the United States of America would experience as an intact nation. After that, who knew? Would the events stop in Hawaii or continue marching west? Obtaining an answer to that question was why he had been loaned to the CIA. On the other hand, maybe the predicted Hawaii event would prove a dud. Maybe it was too close to the Communist axis: Russia, China and North Korea. Too much collateral damage. Enough damage had already been wreaked on the USA, leaving it ripe for whatever nefarious endgame was supposedly about to come into play.

In the far distance, a dot appeared, growing steadily in size in the shimmering heat. Azaga squinted and wiped his eyes to see better. It didn't look like the B2 he was impatiently awaiting. It looked more like one of the new fighters recently deployed at Marine Base Kaneohe, an F35 "Lightening" VSTOL. Kaneohe, however, was on the other side of the island, and the Marines rarely used Hickham. His interest increased further when the fighter slowed its approach and began hovering over a spot a hundred feet in front of him.

The moment the plane touched down, the cockpit slid back revealing two helmeted individuals instead of one like the F35s he'd seen. Even more unusual, when the second person climbed out onto the wing with a large brown briefcase and the flight helmet was removed, the expected man turned into a woman.

Curious, Azaga thought as the male pilot and his female passenger climbed off the plane's wing and walked directly towards him. On the way, the woman paused, awkwardly opening the briefcase and removing an automatic and a loaded clip, which she held up in one hand, showing them to the sun-reddened man standing wide-eyed in front of them.

Curiouser and curiouser, Azaga thought, reaching his right hand instinctively towards his own weapon.

The pilot offered a hand. "Flight Lieutenant Roger Styles, Sir, delivering…"

Koski slipped the weapon and clip back into the briefcase, shifted the helmet and briefcase to her left hand, and thrust an open right hand towards the man in front of Lieutenant Styles. "Cerebrus Agent Susan Koski," she interrupted.

The man sweating profusely before her looked puzzled.

Who the hell are these two? Azaga wondered, hesitating to shake either's hand. The pilot hadn't identified himself as Falk and didn't look at all like the photo he'd been shown at briefing, and he had been led to believe that Falk was a man not a woman. It was never a good sign when pre-arrangements didn't work out.

Must be Falk's CIA liaison, Koski concluded, scanning the discomforted man. Observing him closer, she concluded, *Looks like a mummified roast chicken.*

"Wha…?" the white clothed, sunburned chicken asked, glancing from one to the other of the two wrong people greeting him while grasping the handle of his weapon firmer.

"What news of Falk?" Koski blurted. The mention of Falk's name afforded Azaga instant though limited relief.

"None," replied Azaga cautiously, even more perplexed. "I

was supposed to meet him here. He was *supposed* to arrive an hour ago in a commandeered B2..."

"We were escorting his plane," interrupted the pilot. "It experienced an echo-intersection and went down in the ocean about 200 miles off Oahu..."

"...where he or his pilot, we couldn't tell which, was picked up by a Russian submarine," concluded Koski. "I take it you haven't heard..."

Jesus! What kind of circus is this? Azaga thought. Satisfied nonetheless that the two were genuine, he released his grip on his weapon.

"Ben Azaga, MI5 on loan to the CIA. You're right Agent Koski, I haven't heard any of this. Things here have been... well...complex...what with all the interagency preparations for the next event. Like I said, I was sent to meet Agent Falk and act as his international interagency resource liaison while he was here. It was my understanding that he was to head up a special field operation to locate a couple of foreign agents and hopefully a handler or controller here on the island. The ocean? A Russian submarine?"

Koski's voice broke when she continued, unable as she was to hide her personal concern. "We don't know if it was Falk who was taken. I...we...don't even know if he's alive..."

"I radioed the information ahead about twenty minutes

ago," the lieutenant added, as if trying to mollify Azaga and afford the man some justification for his confusion. "I'm sorry, but I must get back in the air. I have urgent continuing orders…"

"Yes, of course you do," Azaga replied, picking up Koski's briefcase and slipping a free arm under her slumping shoulders. She looked distressed and exhaused. "I can take things from here, lieutenant."

Styles offered the MI5/CIA agent the briefest of salutes. It had been hard on his passenger to witness her companion's jet explode in the ocean in a ball of flame, and worse, to watch helplessly while they backed away from the Russian submarine that had captured one or the other of the plane's inhabitants. There was no indication of the second inhabitant's condition or whereabouts, and the one aggressively taken aboard Russian submarine, for all anyone knew, might already be dead.

Chapter 34

Captain Alexander Konstantine Korovich stared at the limp, wet form tied onto a metal folding chair in the middle of the briefing room. The form was surrounded on three sides by armed Russian "marines"—military-political Spatznatz forces specifically detailed to this newest of fast attack submarines—and wondered what he'd "caught."

It was always risky, on several levels, to surface. Most dangerous was that it revealed one's existence and position. In waters like these, so close to Hawaii, that was never a good thing to do. Besides, his ostensible assignment was to silently gather intelligence, and neither be seen nor engage. Hawaii was the westernmost home to a forward branch of America's Pacific military forces, and that included a fleet of modern, efficient submarine hunter-killers.

His secondary, more secret mission, the one that took him to this dangerous location and forced him to briefly reveal himself, was to find a way of opening a communication back-channel with America.

America's forces were at full alert, and the situation in the USA had become so tense his military superiors felt that any direct communication from Mother Russia right now might cause America's military to reflexively squeeze the hair-trigger. At best, anything coming from Russia at this time would likely be construed a prelude to an overt act of Russian aggression. Another Pearl Harbor. All that being said, he couldn't pass up the opportunity to "save" what seemed to be the pilot of the downed American B2 they'd spotted and been tracking with interest.

The mere presence of a solitary B2 in this part of the Pacific reflected the level of desperation the United States of America had to be feeling, given its state of affairs. For some reason that entirely eluded Korovich and his military superiors, Eurasia and Africa were being spared the crippling incidents that were bringing down the most powerful nation in the world, and, if Russian computer experts were right, after that, Canada, Mexico, and possibly then Central and South America. In summary, the whole of the Americas. In short, he knew he'd not only caught a big one, he'd caught the right one.

It was nonetheless difficult to tell exactly how big or right, given that the man—he assumed it was a man from what he could make out of its general physique enclosed as it was in a wet, bulky, pressurized flight suit and opaque black helmet. The figure hadn't struggled while they hurried it through the hatch into the bowels of the submarine. It didn't struggle now, while the ship's doctor and medic worked to carefully detach the helmet.

"He's breathing, Cap' Korov, Sir," the doctor announced in Russian, inspecting, then laying aside the intriguing helmet. "Cap' Korov," as his crew fondly called him, watched the doctor and his assistant begin cutting off the flight suit of their surprise guest.

Cap' Korov, a squat man with a head of ultra-short, white fuzz instead of hair—rubbed his wiry white chin stubble with a ham of a hand. His rumpled, short-sleeved working uniform looked as if he had worn it constantly throughout the week. He was joined by a tall, thin, officious-looking man in a smartly creased uniform, whose military insignia identified him as the submarine's political intelligence officer. The pair stood next to each other, observing the slowly emerging figure. The two officers' divergent physiques made them look like a cartoon caricature of Mutt and Jeff.

"And what is this you've brought aboard, Korov?" the tall one asked in crisp Muscovite Russian, shaking his head from side-to-side in mock disgust. "We're supposed to be running reconnaissance, not stopping to shop at every American garage sale we happen by."

"I'm not sure, Comrade Grigorov," the captain replied in his signature St. Petersburg accent, scratching his chin and smiling. "But this is what's left of an American B2…"

Grigorov's thin eyebrows joined together and rose in a surprise salute. "An American B2?"

"Of that much I am certain. While following it on radar, we intercepted a 'mayday' and a few moments later an ejection seat appeared on our sonar on surface…"

"The plane, Korov? What of the plane?" interrupted Grigorov greedily.

"Nothing but tiny pieces scattered over a kilometer-wide area, none of which, aside from this man's ejection seat, were large enough show up on our sensors. Of course, we couldn't stay to inspect. We had barely enough time to capture him and hide. An American military VSTOL plane was hovering nearby. I pinged it with our attack radar and we each took off in opposite directions."

"So we are compromised?"

"One can never be certain of the outcome of such an encounter," Korov replied carefully. "But we can surmise from the VSTOL pilot's unwillingness to engage, the quickness with which the plane turned to run, and the direction in which it fled, that it had an agenda even more urgent than recovering one of their own. What, Grigorov, could be that urgent? There's been no sign of military air or surface activity beyond the usual high-readiness preparations. Now why is that, do you suppose, Comrade Grigorov?"

Grigorov shrugged his shoulders conveying his lack of interest in military tactics, instead carefully eyeing the man being stripped to his non-military skivies.

The man's head lolled forward chin to chest, revealing a small stack of papers taped to one side of his chest. Barely able to restrain himself from grabbing the papers and interrogating the captured pilot, Grigorov offered a controlled nod to the medical officer to remove the papers and hand them to him.

The medical officer did as ordered and Grigorov immediately began rifling them. "*Der'mo*, these smell awful! I know sufficient English to recognize that they are not military, Korov," Grigorov announced. "In fact, they seem to make little sense, which suggests to me they're somehow encrypted, which further suggests this man is more than a pilot. I must assume they are intelligence documents, and need to send copies to Moscow immediately for further analysis." Finished perusing the horrid-smelling papers, Grigorov thrust them into the hands of a reluctant seaman waiting at stiff attention on Grigorov's right. The man, who sported radio operator's insignia, turned smartly and left for the radio room clutching the sheaf of papers in two fingers at the end of an outstretched hand.

Grigorov returned his attention to the intriguing and still unconscious man seated before him.

In the absence of any counter-orders from his political intelligence officer, Korov continued, "As I said, the other aircraft flew away in the opposite direction, towards, I presume, one of the many American military bases located in the Hawaiian Islands. I also presume the pilot issued a report stating that we have one of their pilots. By all expectations, the United States military should be scouring the area as we speak, unless, for examle, this man and his 'papers' are a decoy meant to distract us from what was on the VSTOL."

His counterpart nodded but continued staring at the man in the chair.

"On the other hand," Korov continued, "it seems more likely to me that the American military are too preoccupied at this moment to divert resources to search for him. They must be heavily engaged in preparing for the next odd occurrence, and trying figure out how to defend themselves from what everyone expects to be the final blow. As command has pointed out, these strange occurrences seem purposefully designed to individually be too small to be labeled as overt acts of war, yet collectively too complex and damaging to be mere acts of terrorism. It is in their cumulative effects that they are so destructive to a highly integrated digital/electronic society as the USA. As a whole, they are insidiously stripping that nation of its ability to function, while leaving all its natural and industrial resources intact for the taking. In that sense this series of occurrences presents an incredibly powerful opportunity—powerful enough tempt any enemy wanting to acquire its people, land and resources without having to fight. An ingenious advancement on our present *detente*, is it not?

Grigorov continued to stare at the figure in the chair, as if trying to interrogate it telepathically.

"Is it then, Comrade Grigorov, presumptive to assume that their military authorities are simply too engaged at the moment to attempt the rescue of a man who has their ear and whose likely intent was to convey some crucial information? Surely even you couldn't have anticipated coming across a downed *intelligence agent* at just this moment. I'm guessing this man's mission somehow has everything to do with the next occurrence." *And what better backchannel conduit than such a man?* Cap' Korov stated emphatically in his mind.

The doctor cautiously lifted the figure's right eyelid, then the left, checking each eye's response with a pocket flashlight.

The figure in the chair groaned.

"He's coming around," the doctor said, stating the obvious.

"Good," said Korov. The two line officers took a step back to resurvey the man in the chair, then each other, as if testing each's mettle.

"What exactly do you have in mind?" asked Grigorov, resuming his role as submarine intelligence officer, only marginally subordinate to the captain. "If the Americans are, indeed, 'momentarily distracted', that leaves us little time to extract…"

"He's a 'guest', Comrade Grigorov. A 'guest'. As soon as he recovers his senses, I will notify United States Pacific Fleet to advise them of his 'rescue'…"

"What…?" Grigorov interrupted, astounded.

"…and gladly arrange to release him back to his own kind," Korov completed calmly.

The figure in the chair moved. His dazed eyes rolled, focused, then darted warily from one to another of the men around him. The medic opened an emergency first aid kit, and began wiping clotted blood from their 'guest's' face and mixed blood and vomitus from the rest of his body, while the doctor opened a suture kit.

"Amerikan…Agent," Korov addressed the man in broken-English, while slowly approaching the heavily bruised man sitting tensely and testing his restraints. "We…save…from… ocean. "

"The plane? The pilot?" asked Joseph Falk, parsing the room, and noting his flight suit on the floor to the side, little more than a cut pile of strips with the highly advanced flight helmet resting intact on top of the pile.

Noting their 'guest's' concern, Korov continued, "Planc… gone. Pilot…" he shrugged his shoulders while indicating by his facial expression that he shared his guest's pain. "I have… message…for Amerika," he concluded while Grigorov stared at his comrade, dumbfounded.

Chapter 35

It took some time for Falk's head to clear, for Korov to convince Grigorov of the authenticity and primacy of his heretofore secret secondary orders, and to obtain the political-intelligence officer's reluctant cooperation, then, through Grigorov, who spoke much better English than the captain, to better convey his "message" to Falk and the USA.

What Korov had shared regarding his secret secondary objective was true, however, he carefully omitted his tertiary agenda: not only to establish a communications back-conduit between the US and Russia, but to inform the United States that Russia was as surprised by the occurrences as everyone else, and that she had no part in them. In short, Russia didn't want war. There was already shared worry in the Russian government and military command that the occurrences would be attributed to Russia, but equally, that they might not stop at the westernmost border of North America but continue to march across the Pacific and wreak havoc in their nation. To bolster their claim, the Russian government had ordered the military to share everything they knew about the occurrences, which Korov through an astonished Grigorov, assured Falk was substantive. They would do this, Korov qualified, if Falk could assure Russia's President and head of military command that the United States would, in return, stop regarding Russia as the immediate "enemy," and step down the alert level. In addition, in return for sharing information on the event occurrences. Russia wanted the USA to share everything known so far about the especially perplexing *pradazha* or sales accompanying the occurrences.

At Falk's nod of assent, Korov, through an increasingly astounded Grigorov, offered as proof of Russia's goodwill, that prior to the start of the occurrences, Russia had been secretly working on weaponizing a quantum physics phenomenon called 'entanglement'. In the process, they had shared the their work with China in order to enlist the Chinese military's assistance in producing an operational field prototype. The prototype, thought to still be in China, could not, however, be loosed without the necessary 'initiator' which Russian scientists had cautiously withheld from their Chinese colleagues.

Falk's exhausted body reawakened more with each revelation. By the end of the explanation, he wanted to offer

Korov a triply heart-felt thanks, first for rescuing him, second for sharing the information he'd just received, and finally for the offer to work together to resolve the situation for the benefit of the USA, Russia, and, hopefully, the world.

Priority-wise, the most important thing now was for him to report what he'd learned to Stewart. It was likely that the hard-liners in the Pentagon were even now finalizing what actions they were planning to take against Russia, America's proverbial "enemy." Falk desperately needed to pass on what he'd heard to Stewart, so Stewart could vet it and pass it up the chain to the Joint Chiefs of Staff.

That was, of course, assuming that what he was being told was true. Korov's demeanor suggested to Falk that the man *believed* everything he was saying, though not necessarily so, the translating officer. The cold, careful manner in which Grigorov translated what Korov was saying, shouted caution and distrust. On Russian submarines, the political officer, which Grigorov's uniform and brusque manner clearly identified him as, often had secret orders or withheld key information until a critical moment, and was the only crew member who could directly countermand the captain's orders. And it looked to Falk's tired, but activated mind that Korov's sincerity was not shared by his political officer. That spelled trouble.

Falk listened carefully, probing wherever possible, and at the end was still waffling as to whether the pair's declared intent was genuine. In the end, he believed the captain, but couldn't fully convince himself that Korov was not a pawn in a political ruse to defuse or neutralize the threat of a pre-emptive strike by the USA against Russia, leaving Russia to deliver the final blow. It could also be meant to buy time for the fifth occurrence to happen, thereby denying the USA any ability at all to retaliate. Falk *wanted* to believe that, as Korov said, Russia, having been involved in the theory, design and development of the *kvantovaya mashina smerti*, referred to by Russian military scientists by the acronym "KMS," and translated literally, "Quantum Death Machine," was willing to share details about the technology. If true, it would be his, Cerebrus and the USA's first major break.

When questioned further about the weapon's status, Korov, through Grigorov, claimed that Russia had be unable to advanced the prototype, Russia's computing power being insufficient, Russian military research and development having taken a hit in the latest of a succession of increasingly austere budgets, national military priority having sifted from exotic weaponry to rejuvenating Russia's disorganized army and navy.

Questioned about how the device actually worked, Korov replied with difficultly through Grigorov, that it was a 'delivery system' like no other, as the USA could well see. In fact, though "weaponized," it wasn't technically a weapon at all. It was a system capable of instantaneous teleportation, the idea having been gleaned from watching the old American television series, "Star Trek" and its "transporter." It wasn't technically electronic at all, applying instead a unique property of "quantum strangeness."

The field equipment at the starting and ending locations, Grigorov explained, translating Korov's monologue, had to be *exactly* the same in overall mass, structure and function, in order to "synchronize" the two places in their respective "time-spaces."

Hence the 'custom design' look, thought Falk.

The synchronized sites took advantage of a *kvantovoye yavleniye*, a "quantum phenomenon," explained Korov through Grigorov, though the two were beginning to apologize for their lack of ability to fully explain the physics and effect a meaningful translation. Instead, at this point, Korov switched to reassuring Falk that if Falk provided a knowledgeable American scientist, their Russian scientists could better directly convey the details.

When queried about the satellite antennas, Korov, again through Grigorov, explained they were only necessary to synchronize the two spaces, allowing an object placed in either location to momentarily simultaneously appear in both. The object would then equally instantaneously revert back to one object in one of the two spaces. The simultaneous "transfer" as well as the execution of any actions the object was programmed to perform would appear to an observer to happen without taking up any time whatsoever. It didn't matter where the antennae were pointed, only that they were a perfectly functioning part of the equipment. For nationalistic reasons, they had all been positioned to point towards Sirius, the "dog," or "Red" star.

Hence their pointing to nothing located in near earth orbit, thought Falk.

Despite the seeming truthfulness of what had been shared, Falk still harbored the fear that he might be being used to blindside things in Honolulu and, by doing so, strip the USA of it's last opportunity for defense. What he desperately needed was the "knowledgeable American scientist," one who could be trusted with what could very well prove to the most dangerous technology ever created. It would have to be someone who was not just a world-class scientist, but who could be entrusted with such power. It would need, he concluded, to be someone in Cerebrus.

"I need to communicate what you've shared to my superiors in Washington," Falk urged Grigorov.

"With whom exactly do you propose to communicate?" asked the political officer warily.

Falk thought a moment. To reveal the identity of any agent in any clandestine organization was anathema; to give out the identity of the head of Cerebrus, was strictly taboo. Thinking fast, Falk eliminated Stewart, then Koski, assuming that if she hadn't gone down like him, she would be busy searching for the foreign agents and their handlers or controllers—his original task—in anticipation of the next event. Contacting her would also mean revealing the identity of not just another colleague, but, yes, his lover. But he needn't make that decision. While he had frequently trusted her with his life and the fate of the world, she wasn't the "knowledgeable American scientist" he needed.

In his head, Falk quickly ran through the names of the various chiefs of departments and divisions within Cerebrus and came up with only one person who fit the bill: Kate Keenan. She was a department head. She would have direct access to Stewart without Falk having to reveal him. Cerebrus' Chief Technical Advisor was an acknowledged scientist and, from his past dealings with her, one who was completely trustworthy. Revealing her identity would be a serious breach of protocol that would place her in imminent danger, but he was certain that she could handle it.

"Keenan. Kate Keenan. She's a 'knowledgeable American scientist' with access to civilian, military and governmental officials, as well as our best scientists and researchers."

The radio operator, having finished forwarding the images of the papers found taped to Falk's body, had returned after placing the papers in the security safe.

"Take our guest to the communications room," the Political Commissar told the stunned man, "and assist him in making contact with his colleague. And give him back his papers." When the radio operator hesitated, Grigorov added, "Comrade radioman: That is an order!"

The radio operator, mouth open, obliged after receiving Cap' Korov's grave and unexpected nod of assent.

Chapter 36

The private Gulfstream G650ER carrying Kate Keenan was less than two hundred miles out of Honolulu by the time she'd showered, made up, and donned an off-white, silk, two-piece tropical business suit from the closet. *Commanding,* she thought looking at her reflection in the closet's full length mirror. Something inside told her she would need that look to pull off her assignment. When she returned, she would have to thank Stewart.

This was, in fact, her first official Cerebrus field assignment, and given its gravity, Kate hadn't been surprised when she began receiving in flight situation reports—"sit reps"—from Cerebrus' Head of Field Operations, David Hallard, followed by Directors Halsey and Small on the ever-changing international, national and regional political situations. Keenan was awaiting a call from Lou Richards, Cerebrus' Head of External Security, about any security changes, when she was interrupted by the flight attendant.

"Ma'am, I've a call for you," the she announced softly. "It's a radio-communication from the Pacific Ocean not far from where we are now. The instigator is Russian and speaks broken English. He keeps mentioning the name 'Falk'. For security reasons…"

"…I'll take it. Patch it over to me now, and secure this communication as best you can."

"That will mean revealing our position and that you are on board. There is a chance, ma'am, that it's a ruse to gather intelligence information and, if so, to possibly compromise this mission. I can't be responsible for your safety if you…"

"I accept full responsibility. Please make the connection now!"

A moment later, her cell phone rang. Kate held the phone to her ear with both hands, shaking with what would appear to any onlookers as anxiety or fear. But that would be because they didn't know of Kate's strong personal affection for Falk, he having swept her off her feet during their very first encounter. She never knew if her feelings were mutual, Koski having joined Falk as his partner shortly afterwards, and the two of them having been out on one after another assignment since. This situation presented her an opportunity to find out.

"Yes," Kate answered, her throat dry, her hands shaking.

"Falk, here," replied a constantly distorting voice shrouded in static.

"We've been able to establish an emergency encryption protocol, so the line is now secure, ma'am," the co-pilot broke in.

"Falk, is it really you? I was advised that your plane went down and no survivors had been found. I…we…thought…"

"I'm okay. I'm a 'guest' aboard a Russian submarine. The captain assures me that Russia has nothing to do with the events or auctions. He says if I can identify a 'knowledgeable American scientist,' he will put that person in communication with Russian military scientists who have apparently been working on a device that could account for the events. I've been able to loosely corroborate some of what he's said, but I don't know enough quantum physics to be certain this isn't an elaborate counter-intelligence ploy. I need you to…" Falk's voice—Kate felt *certain* it was his—was slowly becoming re-engulfed in static. She *felt* certain, but was she certain enough to trust her life, that of her Cerebrus colleagues and the fate of the USA and possibly the entire world?

"Falk? Falk? Listen! I need you to tell me something so I can confirm your identity. Think. Something only the two of us…"

Falk's voice reasserted itself above the noisy background.

"Operation Finding Kate. It's where we first met. We were quite attracted to each other. You asked about the faint white circle around my left ring finger where one expects a wedding ring. I…"

"Enough! Joe, what do you need? How can I help?" Kate replied, letting out an audible sigh. It had surprised her when he chose to reveal intensely personal details rather than a shared identity code or phrase. Then it occurred to her: Falk doesn't entirely trust his source. He's being careful not to compromise Cerebrus any further than is absolutely necessary. Okay, she would do whatever she could to help, but keep up her guard.

"I need you to stay on the phone, so the folks here can patch you to Russia and the military research team. Then I need you to conclude whether or not what they're saying is valid. When you come to that conclusion, I need you affirm or deny the validity and then contact your superiors and convey *everything you've found out*. If the info is true, I'll then need you to try to convince your superiors to contact the Joint Chiefs and assure them Russia is an ally, not an enemy. Can you do all this?"

"Yes," Kate answered without hesitating. "I'll wait for the patch and, if the information is valid, will convey my assessment to you, and then your message and what I've learned to my superiors. But what about you…?"

"I'm being treated well. As soon as the Russians are convinced we're playing honestly, they said they'll begin working out an 'exit' strategy for me. Kate, the radio-operator is running a finger across his throat meaning…" Falk's voice once again began distorting only to be engulfed completely in static.

"We've lost contact, ma'am," the co-pilot announced.

How am I supposed to validate technical information if we've lost contact? she thought. *All I know is that he's aboard a Russian submarine somewhere 'not too far away'.* Kate was about to call Stewart, when the co-pilot announced over the cabin speaker, "Another call, ma'am, from one of your colleagues. I'll route it, like the other, to your cellular using secure encryption.

"Falk?" Kate answered the moment the call went through.

"Falk?" came a puzzled, too-clear response. "Kate, this is Lou Richards. What? Have you heard from Falk?"

Kate explained as quickly as she could to Cerebrus' Head of External Security about what Falk—she was now convinced it was indeed Falk she'd talked with—had conveyed, and that the communication had broken before the link to the Russian military researchers had been established. She carefully avoided any mention of her feelings for Falk, or that they were one of the reasons she had been quick to accept the dangerous field assignment when Stewart suggested it. True, she wanted her own field mission, but she had to admit that she didn't want to lose the opportunity of meeting Falk and clarifying the attraction to her he'd just insinuated was real. She had been extremely careful to separate her feelings for him after Operation Finding Kate.

She was interrupted in thought and explanation yet again. "Ma'am. I've received another radio signal, this time via a Russian military satellite link. They're waiting."

Lou Richards had heard enough. "You have to follow up on this, but, Kate, be discrete and debrief with Stewart or me as soon as your talk with the Russian military scientists is over. Good luck, and welcome to the field."

Chapter 37

"Seventy-eight degrees, clear and sunny with constant fifteen mile per hour northeast trade winds. Light showers in the mountains in the early mornings and late evenings. Surf on the leeward side of the island is two to three feet with occasional swells to four. Another perfect day in paradise," the television weatherman droned. Koski had just awakened from a quick cat-nap in the quiet of her temporary billet at the Transient Officer's Facility at Pearl Harbor Naval Base. *Must have fallen asleep with the television on,* she mused. It felt good to hear something in this crazy would was "normal" for a change.

In fact, as far as the average Oahu resident was concerned, the events and auctions on the "mainland" might as well be happening on another planet. People in Hawaii seemed to her very insular in their thinking. Right now, they were busy preparing for work, a quick after lunch surf, and, for dinner maybe a picnic at the beach, all as if nothing had or was about to happen. *The joys of children and fools*, she thought enviously.

Having brought only what she'd stuffed into her briefcase, she'd dozed off in yesterday's clothing. Looking forward to taking a quick shower and ironing her rumpled clothes before grabbing a cup of coffee on her way to the multi-agent command post a few blocks away, Koski stretched and yawned. She sorely missed her usual five plus mile morning jog, but then, things had been anything but usual for her during the last few days.

The US Navy had taken the lead in assembling the special Joint Civilian/Military Command Center that was being brought up to speed even before she'd left Fulton, Ohio. Yesterday, upon arriving, Koski had successfully situated herself within the various military, federal, state and county agencies and could at least compliment herself on that. Now would come the harder and more important part for her work: attempting to locate the expected two agents and their handlers or controllers, assuming Honolulu was indeed the next target and that the event process proved the similar to Spokane.

The latter assumption particularly worried her. The Spokane event had occurred in the middle of a high-density urban area, not at an isolated country farmhouse like the others.

Word had reached her that the two agents had been located several hours after the Spokane event, both dead, the "American" one having been shot by the "Oriental" who then ended her own life. There was no evidence that might suggest any extraction plan, but then, government officials had burst in on the remaining agent, and from what had been reported, the Oriental's suicide seemed more impulsive than planned.

Posing as a Chinese student interested in learning English, she and her American friend, had been assigned by an English Second Language school to a matron who routinely offered a two-student "homestay" experience.

The remainder of the event and auction had been in the *modus operandi* of the prior events: There had been another auction near simultaneous with the event. This time the whole weight of the government's collective computer intelligence groups was brought to bear towards identifying the auction's place of origination, the locations from which various "bids" had come, and the trail of the winner's BitCoins. As yet, all the information hadn't yet been processed, leaving more rather than fewer hypotheses, and no really solid information.

Except for a few things: All the Oriental girls it had been discovered had entered the USA between one and two years prior, and records indicated they'd entered using what had proved to be a fake Chinese passport and visitor visa. They had

241

immediately "disappeared" into the population at large. Also, each Oriental agent had entered the USA close to her final destination. A fast analysis by Homeland Security in Hawaii identified roughly twenty thousand Oriental girls with Chinese passports who had entered the USA via Honolulu during the past twenty-four months, two hundred of whom had not exited after their visas had expired. That narrowed the field considerably.

Furthermore, assuming the process would be the same as Spokane, Koski's first priority would be to identify Chinese *homestay* visitors with expired visas. In addition, the homestay placement should include an American girl who appeared to be a close pal. Finally, the home where they were staying should have a recently installed, new satellite antenna. Unfortunately, all the previous antenna installations had proven untraceable. To Koski, that meant the installation had been done non-commercially, which gave further credence to the idea that the two girls at the least had a local handler, most likely the person who installed the antenna. All that was unique enough to work with. It was too bad that, as Stewart had predicted, her replacement had found no further sign of Josh, the boy who had made contact with her then disappeared. The same appeared true of the Spokane girls suspected handler. If one had been present, he or she had disappeared and was dead or gone.

There was still a half day before the next event was expected to occur. Every moment of Koski's time for the next few hours would be focused on directing inter-agency field teams to check out each and every situation that fit the foreign agent's standing criteria.

After showering and running a conveniently supplied steam iron quickly over her clothes, she exited her room for the small cafeteria located near the building entrance. Pouring a cup of syrupy black military coffee into a styrofoam cup and selecting a small croissant that seemed to be calling to her, she was about to sit at one of the few empty tables when a very military looking Naval officer grasped her by the elbow. "Agent Koski? My apologies. I've been sent by Commander of Naval Intelligence at Pearl Harbor. Something's come up. Something you will definitely want to hear."

Chapter 38

Stewart was interrupted while nervously pacing his office in Washington DC by a ring on his cellular. It was out of his pocket and against his ear so quickly he fumbled and almost dropped it.

"Stewart here!"

"WHAT THE HELL ARE YOU DOING GIVING A RUSSIAN SUBMARINE LOADED WITH MISSILES PERMISSION TO DOCK AT THE CIVILIAN PORT OF HONOLULU? What were you thinking…?"

"Whoa, General Cavors. I didn't 'give permission.' I asked Naval Command to grant permission for the submarine to dock at Pearl Harbor and they denied it. The only other place available was the civilian port of…"

"God damn it, Stewart! Didn't I tell you that the President and Joint Chiefs are one step away from a pre-emptive strike against Russia? Didn't I ask you…*beg* you…to identify and inform me of *any* other possible source for this mess we're in? I appreciate receiving the results of your Delphi, but the joint chiefs didn't by into it. Not yet, anyway. In the meantime, how could you direct an *enemy* submarine to dock in exactly the place where it can wreak maximum havoc all around the Pacific Rim, not to mention setting them up in the best possible place to assess for themselves exactly how vulnerable we actually are…?"

"I thought word had gotten to you that agent Falk, whose plane disintegrated over the Pacific, had been rescued and taken to Hawaii aboard that very submarine. Furthermore…"

"Furthermore, you and your whole Cerebrus organization are one step from being deactivated and having your 'assets' chewed out and handed over to NSA!"

"That may be, Sir; however, Falk reports that the captain of the submarine has information that may be crucial in discovering how the events are created and propagated. Another of my agents is, at this very moment, communicating with Russian military researchers who, I've been told, created and developed the theoretical physics necessary to create…"

"Jeeze, Stewart. Things here are about to explode and you pass this on to me as a consequence of *my* calling *you?* But okay, okay. So we've now got a fully functional Russian submarine docked at the civilian port of Honolulu. Tell me the rest! Now!"

"The captain insists that the Russian military were involved in the creation and development of an event generation machine, but Russia never deployed it and isn't behind the events. They, like us, are mystified about the auctions, and are concerned the events and auctions may not stop with Hawaii…"

"That's interesting," General Richard Cavors, Head of the Joint Chiefs of Staff replied in a calmer more controlled manner. "But has it occurred to you that this whole thing might be a ruse to place Russia in the perfect position to take over the USA and all our resources, natural, civilian and military, *without firing a shot?* Even if Russia isn't behind it all, what if they're one of the 'buyers'? What if they're behind *all* the buyers? This is quite a gamble you're taking, I must say, on behalf of America, the President and the Joint Chiefs…"

"Admittedly, I should have kept you better informed, and, yes, it is a gamble…"

"You're damn well right! Are you aware that in the last hour, rumors have surfaced of dissident citizens assassinating government leaders?" demanded Cavors.

"No, I didn't…" began Stewart somewhat mollified.

"Perhaps your friend, Colonel Rellin, has too wrapped up in matters to keep *you* up to date? Our civilian counterparts are totally engrossed in simply stemming the chaos. In fact, city, state and federal governments are no closer maintaining law and order than you are to apprehending these 'foreign agents' and their handlers!"

"The endgame," offered Stewart.

"The endgame?" repeated Cavors. "The endgame? Hell, we still don't even know who started it!"

"General. Falk is one of my best. If he says the Russian submarine captain is genuine, then I believe him. I have a report coming in from a second agent momentarily. She's talking directly with the Russian military researchers who claim to have created the event generator. I'm also expecting a report from a third agent, who's already on the ground in Honolulu. As soon as I know *anything* more, I'll call you personally. For now, please do what you can to assist Falk in setting up what the Russian captain is calling "a back channel" of communication between you and their country's military leaders, and ultimately directly between the two Presidents. This is our only solid lead just now."

"Okay, Stewart. Consider it done; however, no matter how this plays out, I'm holding you *personally responsible…*!"

"I understand, General, and I take full responsibility for my, my agency's and my agent's actions," confirmed Stewart.

Chapter 39

As her plane began to descend from cruising altitude on approach to Honolulu, Kate Keenan listened, aghast at what she was being told by the Russian military scientists through the Russian interpreter. There would be a flurry of Russian, only a little of which she could understand, then a crusty pause followed by the slow, almost mechanical voice of the military linguistic interpreter.

"Maybe ten years ago…yes, ten years…the Russian military…tasked a secret…'think tank' I think you would call it…to theorize a weapon that could…destroy a nation's infrastructure…without harming it's basic resources, including its people. Over."

"A 'weapon'? Over." asked Kate of the disembodied voice on the other end of the crackling but secure line.

"I'm sorry. Exact translation is difficult. Perhaps 'a solution' or 'an approach'…the idea was to theorize a weapon or solution or approach…that could take the place of nuclear weapons. Mutually Assured Destruction—MAD—was never a solution acceptable to our military leaders. Over."

"And they came up with…?" Kate probed.

"They came up with…the *kvantovaya mashina smerti*…the KMS…the 'Quantum Death Machine'…which our researchers here believe is being deployed against the United States of America. Over."

"How exactly does it work? Over," Kate demanded.

"Assembled perfectly…it must be *twice*-perfect…I will explain that later…it becomes a…specialized quantum…ah… teleportation device. When…awakened…even for the shortest time…less even than a formal 'jiffy'—the amount of time light takes to travel one fermi, about the size of a nucleon, in a vacuum—an object from one place will appear simultaneously in another predetermined, linked location. Distance doesn't matter. Only the…fixing…of the two points in absolute time-space. It was based on…no, inspired by…the thought-experiments of the Austrian physicist Erwin Schrödinger in 1935. He proposed a thought experiment…later called 'Schrödinger's Cat'…in which, given the 'rules' of quantum mechanics…a cat inside a box could, for the briefest of moments, be…both alive and dead at the same time. Over."

"You mean *actual teleportation?* Over," asked Kate.

"Everyone here is shaking their heads 'no'...not *real* teleportation. For just an instant the object...it appears in two places simultaneously. For just instant. Then...depending on how equipment and object are...manipulated...'programmed' would be a better word one researcher says...another says to remind you that no programming is actually necessary at all... at least within the system itself. The two perfectly matched sites are...completely passive in the electronic sense...as would be an unprogrammed object. And the device... remember, there must be two of them...a duality, you see...one at at each site...they must be as I said, *perfect* copies. The device must be *twice* perfect. In order for a twice perfect system to work...the two devices must be precisely located in absolute space-time...for that particular instant. This requires considerable...computational skill and power. Over."

"Indeed," Kate agreed. "The world we experience every day *seems* fixed to us, but, in fact, everything in the universe, including our world and us upon it, even our universe itself, is constantly moving, in one or another direction, at one or another speed while time marches on. Fixing two points in space-time would be *extremely* challenging. I don't know that its ever actually been done. Over."

"Yes, this proved the most challenging part...of moving theory to physical prototype. We...that is, this group of scientists here…needed more computing power than was available at that time in Russia…so we…they…turned to the Chinese, with their…Tianhe super-massive computer. 'Tainhe' means 'Heaven River' or 'Milky Way.' The world knows the 'Tianhe-1A' as the fastest computer that has ever existed, but our…Chinese military comrades…had in their possession another…already ten or more generations more advanced. Our leaders agreed to share the workings of the KMS, the *kvantovaya mashina smerti* or Quantum Death Machine in return for use of their advanced Tianhe, their…top secret super-massive military computer…to calculate the simultaneous space-time coordinates necessary to perform an actual… ah…'proof of concept' you would say. Over."

"A working Quantum Death Machine actually exists in China? Over."

"Well, yes…and no. We built the prototype…they provided the necessary coordinates for a test…but we never completely trusted our Chinese comrades…more so the North Korean military scientists who were there working side-by-side with the Chinese…so we provided the prototype machine, but withheld the….'initiator'. Over."

"Were the 'tests' successful? Over," asked Kate.

"Again, yes and no. We were able to make a molecular sized object…simultaneously appear in another place…but had difficulty making it stay at the desired location. Most often the...object of interest...simply vanished after momentarily appearing in the place where we directed it. This made it of... less interest...to our military leaders, since consistent 'delivery' of a larger payload could not be assured. Over."

"What happened to the prototype? Did the Chinese advance it further? Are they behind this, do you think? Over," requested Kate.

"The prototype and initiator were destroyed...by the very scientists standing about me...of this, they are certain. However, having further considered their time there, they now think the Chinese may have successfully built a *copy* of the *kvantovaya mashina smerti*—less, of course, our initiator which we never revealed. This copy, our scientists believe, would likely be a system of interconnected modular elements...a dual copy, hand-crafted to correct for the... deficiencies...in the prototype...in order to continue their investigations. It would likely consist of numerous interconnected boxes..."

"So you think the Chinese are behind this? Over."

"You Americans are always...so direct. No, we, that is, the scientists standing around me, don't think so. According to Russian intelligence, the Chinese never...figured out...how to recreate the initiator. Besides, what exactly would they 'deliver' with this device? Aside from being…an instantaneous way of delivering a small…currently less than three centimeter object —it can not be larger due to the inherent 'rules' of Quantum Simultaneity—how could they be certain what they delivered would remain at the delivery point…and not end up remaining at—you may also think of it as 'returning to' if you like—the source point. Were it even possible to create, say, a microminiture nuclear weapon…how could they be assured they wouldn't obliterate everything at the point source and leave instead in their their enemy's hands one of the required dual systems to take apart and learn from? Over."

"Then what exactly are you saying? Over."

"We believe North Korea to be responsible for these… events. North Korean scientific and military observers worked next to Russian and Chinese military scientists. They saw and examined the original prototype…our intelligence service believes they remained on the project for several years helping the Chinese devise the Chinese prototype. We believe that…the Chinese, unsuccessful at creating a working initiator… abandoned the project and the North Koreans returned to their country…to, we believe, create their own version. The problem still remains that…one, they still didn't have an initiator…and, two, they had no idea at the time what to 'deliver'. Over."

"At the time?" Kate inquired. "At *what* time? Over."

"Yes, but now we believe…they have solved both problems and…identified a 'use' for the KMS. Over."

"And?" demanded Kate.

"We believe their military researchers…have devised a way to create an occurrence…an 'event', as you call them…by tearing a rent in space-time at the target location…with assurance. That is, they deliver not an object, but the occurrence or event. The scientists here believe what you are experiencing is the result of the momentary creation of a…'special singularity'. Over."

"A *tiny* 'Big Bang'?" asked Kate, quickly coming to believe what she was hearing, and now more interested than ever.

There was a pause on the other end, during which the researchers there engaged in an audible debate.

"I'm sorry. There is considerable disagreement here about that. Some say, yes, it is an artificial 'Big Bang'…but one that is…tightly 'contained'. The detractors point out that…the technology for containing even a *nuclear* explosion…still doesn't yet exist…and, anyway, why, they argue, would North Korea care if the 'Big Bang' were…contained…or not? To this, another group here replied…that containing it would resolve the problem of the event happening only where it's directed… instead of possibly at the source. To which an opposing group is arguing that under any circumstances…anything present within a small…'location zone' would simultaneously appear at both…and remain at one or the other. Whether contained or not, it's a fifty percent phenomenon…'quantum mechanics'… they are all yelling at each other here, so perhaps I am translating this incorrectly and it doesn't work exactly that way. Still, the North Koreans must have figured out how to make the occurrence non-statistical…not unprovable…sorry, I should have said 'no longer unpredictable'. So there you have it. Over."

There I have it, thought Kate. Instigator, method, and purpose. "Our scientists have been experimenting with artificially-created 'Big Bangs'…" she offered in return.

"Yes. Everyone is. According to…M-Superstring Theory… if one can…posit…the right circumstances in all eleven-dimensions of space-time, one can create using the *kvantovaya mashina smertia*…and teleport a 'Big Bang'."

Indeed, thought Kate. The 'bang' would be instantaneous. Before it would be noticed, the rent in space-time would collapse, instantaneously disappearing from our world, leaving a "new" universe pinched off from ours to grow side-by-side, forever unnoticed. M-Supersting Theory, in fact, predicted this. However, before the new universe pinched off, it would create an event-echo of it in our space-time exactly as was being observed. Nothing would be left pointing to its ever having happened. Just the hand-made, modularized machinery and perhaps a special antenna to synchronize the two points in time-space, allowing the translocation of the 'bang' from the first location to the second.

"But why the auctions? Over," asked Kate aloud, as much to herself as to the scientists on the other end of the line.

The person on the other end translated this to the scientists. After some discussion, he replied, "All of this…the scientists here…it's impossible to translate exactly what they are saying…they 'speculate with certainty' that…the 'auctions', as you call them, would be a purely North Korean phenomenon. Relying as they do so heavily on an extensively developed cyber-warfare expertise…I'm sorry, but the political officer standing next to me…is warning me that…such a statement as I have just made…is outside the bounds of our discussion. The group has shared with you everything they can."

Any more, Kate thought, *would actually be superfluous*. She had enough to certify the veracity of the information she'd received and assure everyone technical it was genuine. While doing so, her thoughts began racing ahead, thinking of possible ways to thwart the upcoming event, and a concept of exactly how to do it was already forming in her brilliant, fertile mind.

Chapter 40

Stewart received Kate's summary of her discussion with the Russian military scientists with a sigh of relief. If he was to believe Falk, the Russian submarine captain and Kate Keenan, Cerebrus' New Technology Advisor and all-round science and computer genius, then this was the breakthrough he'd been so nervously awaiting. It would mean that the "enemy" was no longer invisible. It meant that he had both the why *and* the how behind the events, and a first glimpse into North Korea's endgame. As for the auctions, Stewart had already been near certain that North Korea was behind them, though he still needed actual proof in order to present the information to his long-time friends and colleagues, Colonel Jack Rellin, Cerebrus' liaison to NSA, and General Richard Cavors, Chairman of the Joint Chiefs, the "brains" and the "brawn" respectively of America. Still, the information he now possessed was significant. And, he had Kate's assurance that she already had the makings of a countermeasure in mind, one, she had assured him, that was already well tested and, given some quick work regarding the particulars necessary to apply it in this specific situation, was available for deployment.

What he still desperately needed was *proof* that North Korea was behind both events and auctions—hard, explicit proof—and for this, he needed his Honolulu field team, namely Falk, Koski, and Kate to capture an agent, handler or controller alive.

Chapter 41

Koski took a quick sip of the potent military coffee, and left it and her pastry to make her way to the *ad hoc* Ops Center. Her plan was to get updated—that's what the Commander of Naval Intelligence's aide had been sent to call her in for—and then immediately begin deploying the field investigation teams. Time was of the essence, and without Falk, she was on her own. Not that being in charge bothered her that much; she and Falk had always shared equally in devising field plans, and she felt no less adept now than before.

What was bothering her like a stone in her shoe was Falk's absence. She knew he was alive—she'd celebrated his "rescue" alone in her room with a flood of tears that she couldn't hold back. He was, she reassured herself, in "enemy," albeit "friendly" enemy hands, and, having successfully established a back channel of communication between Russia and the USA, he would, she assumed, be soon released. The news of the

Russian submarine docking at the Aloha Tower pier in Honolulu had spread like wild-fire, totally eclipsing public concern over what locals were celebratorily calling the impending "non-event." The populace had, in the last year survived three non-hurricanes, two non-tsunamis and a non-volcanic eruption. In each case, the public had been "prepared to da max," only to experience two usual tropical depressions with the usual moments of blinding, pounding rain; two tsunamis, the largest one only six inches above mid-tide; and yet another unfelt eruption of Kilauea that, in the end, barely received mention the next day. *Thank God the populace here doesn't understand that much about what's happening, especially the intensely critical nature of the coming event.* Koski thought. *The endgame. That's what both Falk and Stewart had deemed this one. Thank God it's happening in Hawaii, where most citizens this morning were more concerned about the surf and whether to take a drive to Aloha Tower to see the submarine.*

And thank God that Falk is alive. Now if only he were here…

Falk, she was no longer reluctant to admit, had become more than her "other half" in more ways than she could recount. When he was with her, she *felt* his presence, his calm, his deep sense of duty, his focus, his concern…and admittedly, his protective love, for that was what it was: love. Pure and simple. Standing on the steps leading up to the Ops Center, she paused, took a deep breath, envisioned him, and let her breath out slowly. He might not be here in the flesh, but she could vividly imagine him walking up the stairs at her side, the two of them planning out the day's work together.

Passing through the glass doors, she glanced behind her as if to say goodbye to the all-too-quickly fading mental image of her lover, and bumped into someone. Hoping it wasn't some high-ranking military officer, she was surprised to see Kate Keenan, kneeling, picking up the papers that had dropped from her hands as a consequence of their encounter. "Kate! What are you doing here?" Koski asked incredulously.

"Picking up what you so ignominiously knocked from my hands. It was my morning briefing. I don't know if I can get them all back in order before…"

Kate Keenan looked bright, confident, smelled like a freshly picked flower and was dressed to the hilt, causing Koski to look down and survey herself. Her clothes still looked rumpled and she was sure they smelled of having been previously worn and, last night, slept in. She felt anything but confident and could only imagine the puffiness about her eyes after her night's cry and how bloodshot they probably looked after only a few hours of real sleep. For some reason it disturbed her more than it should have.

"Glad to see you," Koski said, consciously softening her voice. "With Falk almost dying and still gone, I'm in charge of the entire field operation including pre-pinpointing the event's epicenter and, if possible, capturing the two agents."

"Which is why *I'm* here," replied Kate with command and authority. "I've been talking with the Russian military scientists who created the prototype device that causes the transmigration of a spatial-temporal rift from one location to another via quantum entanglement…"

"Have you talked to Falk?" Koski asked, interrupting, not wanting to have to ask Kate what exactly she was talking about.

"Yes," Kate answered, aggravated at having her rehearsal cut off.

"Did he sound okay? I mean…"

"Yes. In fact, he sounded fine. What's…?"

"I'm sorry. Your talk with Russian scientists," Koski offered, "does this mean that you know how the events are created?"

"Yes, I do," stated Kate haughtily, the question, *Why don't I like this person?* running reflexively through and around her mind. "And I may have a way to stop this one from happening, but I need to be at the event epicenter *before* it happens."

"So you'll be working with me, then?" asked Koski, gathering her wits and, as Falk would do, refocusing on the problem, thinking, *Why don't I like this person?* but saying, "I don't think we've *formally* met…" The inanity of her comment took a moment to strike the two women, causing each to involuntarily cringe.

"That's probably because we *haven't formally* met, though I know about you, and you have most likely heard about me from Falk." Kate offered a hand. Koski didn't return the gesture. People were coming in and going out of the center, flowing around the two as if the women were a couple of rocks in a the center of a rushing stream.

"Falk?" repeated Koski with suspicion. "No, he never mentioned you." He had, of course, but long after Koski and Falk had met and become a team. "But I know of you from reading the summary of Operation Finding Kate. I assume then that they 'found' you…?"

Kate laughed and extended her hand once again. "The 'affair' was given that name *ex post facto*, and, yes, I was 'found'. And later recruited by Cerebrus. And don't let my clothes deceive you. I've been field trained." It wasn't a complete lie. She *had* completed field agent training, but her technical and administrative skills kept taking precedence over any actual field work, so, in fact, she'd not yet taken part in a field operation. "In case you're wondering, I'm the head of Cerebrus' Advanced Technology Division. It's so advanced and secret, I'm supposed to kill you having mentioned it. Perhaps that's why our paths haven't crossed until now."

The satire wasn't lost on Koski. This time, she took Kate's hand and shook it, though she felt strongly off-put at Kate's use of the word "affair" to describe Operation Finding Kate and the inherent threat in the use of the word "kill." Initially, Kate's grip felt overly strong, like she was trying to establish dominance. But then the woman's grip lessened, leaving Koski without a reason to adjust the strength of her grip accordingly.

"Who 'found' you exactly?" asked Koski, wanting to put Kate back in her place.

"Actually, I found myself. That is, I figured the way out of my dilemma. To be completely honest, Joe 'rescued' me, though it was afterwards. Ever since, I've had stars in my eyes and a place in my heart for that man, but that's a different story altogether."

Now I know why I don't like her, thought Koski. That would mean Falk 'knew' Kate, whatever that meant, well before he 'knew' her in the way that usually meant. The thought toughened her, and Koski extended to her full height, her mind questioning, *Why am I doing this? So Falk had a prior relationship; most people did. Wasn't that to be expected?*

266

It's because the woman standing across from me oozes confidence and is being overbearing, her mind replied.

Having sparred and established a mutual wariness and dislike for each other, the two women smiled and walked together from the stream of people into the briefing room.

"The briefing I'm supposed to give is actually more for you than anyone else. Stewart asked me to work in parallel with or as part of your field team. As soon as you locate the upcoming event epicenter, I can begin my 'counterstrike'."

The briefing was short and to the point.

Kate disclosed only enough to establish that she had significantly advanced the technology that had gotten her into trouble in Operation Finding Kate, such that instead of "passively receiving the event," she felt reasonably certain she could counter it with "exactly what the perpetrators are wishing for." The "something," she assured, was being weaponized in her division laboratory in Washington DC even as she spoke.

Towards the end of the short joint agency briefing, a commotion arose in the back of the conference room. Koski peeled her angry gaze from Kate and looked to discover Falk standing there dressed in a Russian seamen's garb. Falk, catching Koski's eye, smiled, shrugged his shoulders and raised his hands, as if apologizing for the plane crash, his unannounced arrival and unusual attire.

Koski's jaw dropped and she stared open mouthed at Falk. She couldn't help but think the man standing at the other end of the room was *the* most appealing man she had ever laid eyes on, and wanted to rush to him, throw her arms about him and show him just how much she cared.

Instead, she laughed circumspectly at his appearance. In his Russian sailor clothes, he really did look silly. Then, out of the corner of her eye, she noticed Kate also staring at Falk with an obvious, dreamy, longing in the woman's eyes. *She's not at all surprised at seeing him*, Koski observed, concluding, *so she must have known he was coming to the briefing but withheld that during our short tête-à-tête*. If Koski disliked Kate before, the resentment she had been feeling upped her dislike to outright disdain.

It was Falk who, extricating himself from the clamor of well-wishers, walked up to and stood comfortably beside Koski rather than Kate. "It's good to see you, Koski," he ventured, turning a lock of her hair in his fingers.

"It's good to see you, too, Falk," she responded quietly, in an attempt to keep their conversation between the two of them. "It's *so* good to see you. It looks like the Russians treated you well."

"The fact is, they saved my life. I hadn't fared well during the flight, and when the plane experienced an unanticipated intersection, I damn near died. The pilot still hasn't been found. If it hadn't been for Captain Korov being in the right place at the right time with the right orders, I wouldn't be here beside you."

"But you *are* here," Koski affirmed, taking his hand in hers and squeezing it. "And you look downright sexy in that Russian naval uniform."

"Uh…yes," replied Falk, suddenly looking the awkward boy. "We barely begin a life together and this happens. It's exactly what I've been concerned about from the beginning: Our work, Koski, is so dangerous, and it will always be getting between us. Either one of us may end up dead anytime. That was my second to the last thought before I blacked out in the water. My last was simply of you."

Falk smiled warmly and Koski returned the same.

"But right now, I've got to talk with Kate," he continued, his smile fading. "I need to know what she was able to make of what the Russian scientists shared. She needs to quickly locate…"

"…the epicenter of this next event, assuming it is indeed in Honolulu and not Alaska," Koski finished for him. "She told me she has a possible countermeasure, but that it requires her to be at the epicenter before the event occurs. She'll therefore be working 'closely' with us in the field, traveling with us wherever we go."

Falk thought for a moment, weighing the implication as much as the content of what Koski had just said. Koski, he ventured, had been acting strangely from the moment he saw her. He was certain it had something to do with whatever it was she *wasn't* saying, but whatever it was, it was totally eluding him. Taking a chance, he added, "No problem. Kate's a trained field agent as well as a talented scientist and a genius with applied physics and things computational. It'll be good to have her with us. We might…"

"There was more than simple 'comradery' in Kate's eyes when you appeared. Do you two have a history?"

"Well, yes, in a way," Falk explained, suddenly cognizant of what was likely going on based on where their conversation had suddenly digressed. "I met her immediately after Operation Finding Kate and based on what I'd leaned of her, recommended her to Stewart. But no, we have no history as lovers."

Koski palpably relaxed.

So Koski, his "partner" was feeling jealous? It wasn't uncommon for paired agents, especially those "with a history" to react overly emotionally immediately before or after a life-threatening situation, and this one was life-threatening for everyone American. "Really, I must talk with Kate. Would you like to accompany me?" Falk asked in all honesty.

Koski affirmed her desire to accompany Falk with a slight nod, and walked hand-in-hand with him over to Kate.

As he'd stated, he and Kate exchanged information. In the end, all three shook hands in acknowledgement of their forced trio-ship, Koski noting with concern Kate's attempt during the handshakes to hold Falk's hand distinctly longer than propriety required. Of more concern to Koski, however, was that Falk didn't make any visible attempt to break the longer-than-needed physical contact with Kate. *They may not, as Falk assured, 'have a history'* thought Koski, *but they damn well have something!*

Chapter 42

The new field team of Koski, Keenan and Falk spent the next hour pouring over and collating everything that had been gathered about visitors from China, English-Second-Language schools and students in homestay. Using a composite description of the previous girls and another of the antennas, calls for public assistance were issued by participating agencies to be carried on radio, television and social media sites in Hawaii.

Their next task was more difficult: prioritizing the list of names and addresses that resulted from their effort, and working out a schedule for each of the twenty or so inter-agency field teams, Koski, Keenan and Falk reserving the most likely sites to visit themselves. While Koski and Falk worked out the final details of the schedules, Kate called her laboratory in Washington DC to confirm that the countermeasure device was on its way directly to her to Honolulu.

It was a warm, cloudless morning, promising temperatures in the high 80s with a heavy UV exposure for the unprotected, and as yet it was only ten o'clock. It would be a scorcher by three, the computer-predicted time of the upcoming event. That left the team less than five hours to locate a Chinese-Asian agent from among the many Chinese in the "Rainbow State." Sadly, residents and visitors alike typically appeared to "mainland" eyes as all Oriental, so the presence of an Oriental girl, even one holding hands with an American female companion would be quite commonplace. Strike one.

The forty ESL schools on Oahu had been fully cooperative. Unfortunately sixty to seventy percent of their students were Oriental, about thirty percent of whom identified themselves as Chinese. Most of the schools maintained files on their students, especially the Chinese for visa reasons, and many maintained a homestay registry. Some, however, did not. Collating all the information together narrowed their search to slightly less than two hundred potential homestay sites with some omissions due to missing data. With less four hours to go, it would be difficult to impossible to visit and carefully interview each. Strike two.

Further, not all students would homestay through an ESL-affiliated school, and non-school-affiliated homestays would prove much more difficult to identify. In fact, of visitors who chose homestay *without registering at an ESL school*, by far most were "Oriental," albeit "Chinese females." "If they aren't accepted at premiere schools in their own country, oriental boys," it was explained, "irrespective of their academic prowess, are often second-choice shipped off to the USA to bolster their English and attend an American college or university. Academically-gifted girls, on the other hand, are generally given a non-school-affiliated English language homestay in Hawaii as a 'consolation prize'." Placement of the foreign agents in out-of-the-way country locations had reflected the general need for secrecy. In a more urban setting like Honolulu, a non-school-affiliated homestay seemed quite likely.

The list of "consolation" homestay sites had proved surprisingly extensive. Adding these to their list of ESL-school-affiliated homestays resulted in two *thousand* possible sites, with an increased number of omissions. Strike three.

By two thirty, the team had cross-indexed the two hundred Chinese girls who had not returned to China after their visas had expired with the various homestay permutations and whittled the number of site visits to less than a hundred. With twenty teams that meant five site visits each with Koski, Kate and Falk reserving the mostly likely for themselves. It was during this time that Kate received the package she'd ordered from her laboratory. It proved a surprisingly compact, nondescript "black box" that fit comfortably in the palm of her hand. Base hit.

Their break came when a Makiki neighborhood area resident living not far from the University of Hawaii at Manoa responded to one of the public service announcements. He called in to report the appearance of a new satellite antenna in a neighboring house, at which two good-looking girls, one Oriental and one "*haole*"—meaning Caucasian in local pidgin —were staying.

Minutes later, the threesome were sitting in a car a block from a nondescript blue and white split level house sandwiched between two similarly constructed but differently colored houses.

From the public sidewalk to the main door of the house was a short twenty feet; the spaces between the sides of the houses appeared, at most, fifteen. Each house looked to have a small backyard, this particular one surrounded by a four-foot-high chain-link fence with the fence gate conveniently dangling open.

The house and yard in question appeared maintained. There was a single "island car," a dented Toyota station wagon with a surfboard rack, parked on the street immediately in front of the house. The house's roof featured a satellite dish antenna that was relatively new in appearance and not dissimilar from the ones Koski and Falk had encountered at their sites.

"This might or might not be the epicenter," Kate, examining the blasé house with obvious disinterest, ventured.

"We should pay them a visit, nonetheless," reminded Koski. "We're near the university. Its a good place for our two girls to blend in. Even if it's not the right place, perhaps whoever lives there has seen or knows something…"

"You're right, of course, Koski," Falk agreed, a little too quickly and assuredly for her. "We're nearing three o'clock, and none of the other teams have turned up anything better. The governor has just issued a call for residents to remain in their workplaces and home, to turn off and disconnect all electrical devices, and not drive. Emergency Services are on highest alert. The National Guard is poised to quell any resulting civil disturbances. Our combined military forces are ready to respond to any identifiable threat." As he talked, all of Honolulu, normally a boisterous city, abruptly fell silent.

Kate slipped the black box into her pocket, and the three prepared to leave the car to interrogate the house's inhabitants when the sound of a single gunshot broke the silence and echoed loudly down the street.

All three huddled reflexively behind respective car doors.

Gunshots, thought Falk, pulling out his weapon, clicking off the safety and chambering a round.

Definitely a handgun, thought Koski, pulling out her weapon, clicking off the safety and chambering a round. *Just like at the Thorsdan ranch in Fulton.*

Good God! We may have actually stumbled onto the epicenter! thought Kate, pulling the diminutive black box back out of her pocket and shifting it to her left hand while grasping her weapon tightly in her right. She was surprised to notice that the palm of her gun hand was damp.

The three agreed to approach the house from different directions, Falk reminding everyone that their priority was to take the agents alive if at all possible. Capturing their handlers or controllers would come later, assuming they could take at least one of the two girls alive.

On Falk's signal, slinking out from behind the car's front passenger side door, Koski ran in a crouch behind and to the back of the residents' old parked car. Kate, at the same moment, ran from behind the back passenger side of their car in an arc to the right to the chain link fence. Falk ran from behind the driver's door, around Koski and up to the front door of the house, where he flattened his body against the paneling to the side of the door, his gun ready. While knocking and announcing himself, two more shots rang out. *Small caliber Type 77 handgun*, he mused, *like the one at the Hempsted farm.*

The two shots, like the first one, all came from inside the

house and apparently weren't directed at him or his companions. Given what he'd seen in Vermont, the shots probably meant at least two persons had just met their death, the first, most likely the homestay parent with one shot. The question was, whether the remaining two were directed at the Oriental's companion, or one at her leaving the second one to be self-directed by the shooter.

Falk signaled for Koski to approach the other side of the front door. As she ran, Koski signaled for Kate to slip through the fence gate, and cover the back entrance.

The moment Koski joined Falk, he swung around to face the door, kicked it open and swept the room, his weapon braced in both hands.

The living room was appointed "island-style" with worn, rattan furniture that had probably been purchased from a second-hand hotel outlet. It looked unoccupied. The sofa was situated to look out two windows onto the small front lawn. A modest entertainment center, a well-used, overstuffed, leather low-boy chair and the open front door occupied the rest of the space between either of the windows. An old surfboard stood upright in a corner of the room.

A rustle sounded upstairs.

Falk signaled for Koski to search the adjoining kitchen while he crept stealthily up the worn, carpeted stairs.

What Koski discovered in the kitchen was what she expected, given her experience in Fulton: A middle-aged man with lightly greying temples was sitting in a kitchen chair, arms, legs and head splayed limply out. He was wearing a white airbrushed t-shirt and blue shorts. His shoes, a pair of island flip-flops, had fallen off his feet when he was thrown backwards. Blood was pooling about the chair's two back legs. The kitchen table and appliances behind him were polka-dotted with bright red.

At the top of the stairs, Falk paused, facing the length of a hallway, noting an open door on his left, waiting for release from the *deja vu* that was haunting him of having been in this same situation before.

Premonition?

Falk pointed his weapon at the open door and proceeded cautiously forward.

Lying in the center of the bedroom floor was the body of a young American girl, blood streaming from a high left neck wound and and another on her left thigh. Crouching lower, scanning the room and not seeing the expected Asian counterpart or any equipment or antenna wire, he knelt beside the limp figure and pressed two fingers against her neck artery. Locating a definite pulse, he thought, *She's still alive, though not for long without emergency care,* noting next, how odd it was that her partner, undoubtedly a highly trained professional like all the other Oriental agents, had botched the killing.

A noise from the hallway bought his survival senses into high gear, and he turned, swung up his weapon, braced and pointed it at the doorway. Two dark silhouettes flew from right to left outside the doorway, from what little he saw, both females, both crouching, each holding before her a weapon that in outline looked remarkably like a standard Cerebrus-issue automatic.

Falk sighed, thinking it had to be Koski and Keenan attempting to back him up, then he abruptly sucked in his breath when he heard three loud concussions, one immediately after the other, ostensibly from the hallway and saw one silhouetted figure fly this time from left to right and out of his sight. The remaining dark figure jumped into the room in which he was crouching and, pointing her weapon at the doorway, turned a pale face towards Falk.

"Oh, God, Falk! I think I just shot another human being!" replied Kate breathlessly, her face and knuckles turning whiter by the moment. Clutching the black box in her left hand and her smoking weapon in her right, she moaned, "Oh, God! Oh God! Oh…"

"Kate! Stop!" demanded Falk. "Are you hit? What about Koski?"

Kate looked dazedly at Falk, then at the barely breathing girl lying beside him in an ever-increasing pool of blood. "Oh, God! Oh, Falk!" she exclaimed reaching out for him, pausing in mid-reach to declare, "I think I'm going to faint."

"Not now!" Falk commanded. "Focus! What about Koski?"

"Koski?" Kate repeated distantly, eyes already glazing.

"Damn it woman! Shake it off! Remember your training! Put down your weapon and the box, and press one hand on this girl's neck wound and the other on her thigh wound. If she stops breathing, give her CPR. We need her alive!"

Kate, despite her unfocused eyes, dropped her weapon onto the floor and placed the black box delicately next to it.

"The event, Falk!" she exclaimed as she reached for the girl's body, her color slowly returning as she refocused her attention onto the wounded girl. "Falk! It's about to happen! The box! We've got to locate the event equipment!" she exclaimed. Pointing to the box beside her gun with her nose, she continued, "That box needs to be inside the room when the event happens. Do you hear? It's got to be inside the…"

Falk scooped up the box in his blood-stained free hand. "What do I do with it?"

"Nothing," Kate replied, recapturing some semblance of calm at last. "Just make certain it's in the room when the event happens."

Falk was out the door and into the hallway before Kate finished. Facing the end of the hallway, gun in one hand, the small black box in the other, he now faced one of the most difficult decisions of his life: whether to backtrack down the stairs to check on Koski—he couldn't see or hear her or to plunge ahead and make certain the black box was in the room at the right moment. His choice, however, was opted by a an even more urgent mental question. *Which room?* There were three closed doors, one on his left near the end of the hallway, and two on his right. While staring forward, searching heart and soul, he heard a familiar voice behind him and felt Koski's hand on his right shoulder.

"Koski, are you alright?" he whispered, not daring to take his eyes off the hallway.

"Good enough...to back you up," she whispered. Her words were clear, but she seemed breathless and was gripping onto his shoulder tightly as if something were wrong. The hand gave a little squeeze, then let go.

"Damn it, Koski! You're hurt!" Falk exclaimed, rescanning the hallway in front of him, in the process noting a spattering of red on the left side of the far wall and what looked like a trail of red dots leading to the single closed door on the left. Kate's shot must have indeed connected with its target.

"I just said, 'I'm good enough to back you up'. Now go,

Falk! I'll cover you."

Falk dropped low, and half-crawled his way to the closed door on his left. Squatting, he looked momentarily back down the hallway from where he'd come. Where he'd just been, he could make out the top of Koski's head, her body flattened against the carpet, both arms extended forward grasping her automatic, a gash of red where her left temple hair should have been. Hearing a noise, he returned his attention back to the door.

There was movement inside the room. It sounded like someone shuffling about carrying something. If so, then this would be the time to enter. Hopefully the Oriental agent would be pre-occupied with whatever final actions were needed before the event happened. He stood and violently kicked open the door.

Inside, below the far window, he could see a table with several rows of inter-connected metal boxes much like the ones he had seen in Laplacia. The window was open. A long cable snaked through it onto the table. A short, thin girl with long, jet black hair had her back to him. Startled by the noise, she dropped the box she was carrying onto the table, and without looking back, shoved the end of the cable into a receptacle of the box she had dropped and the connector of the wire from another box into it. The right side of her patterned dress, Falk observed, was soaked with what was unquestionably blood.

He was about to shout, when she flipped a switch, spun about, and pointed her weapon at him. Three shots shook the room, the first from just behind Falk, the second from the girl's weapon, and the third from his.

Falk heard the whizz of a bullet pass from behind and over his shoulder, watching it strike the surprised girl in the center of her chest. The blow threw her backwards against the table, jarring the table's contents. The boxes were humming, responding to the jolt with countdown beeps, the light next to the switch the girl had thrown changing from flashing yellow to constant red.

The same instant, Falk felt a hard slap, as if he'd been punched in the upper left side of his chest by a bareknuckled prizefighter. Momentarily stunned, he watched the girl jerk a second time, and scream with mixed pain, fear and rage, her left arm twisting and flailing backwards out of control.

Falk didn't wait for her to fire again. He tossed the small black box into the room and, with all his strength, heaved himself out.

To Falk's surprise, the impending event occurred without flash or bang. The constant red light on what seemed to be the master control box simply went out, the humming ceased, and the black box he'd tossed lay inert on the ground.

From the hallway, Falk could see the girl holding onto the edge of the table behind with her right hand without letting go of the gun, while she gasped, eyes wide, lips twisting into a sudden snarl. Letting go of the table, she began falling to the floor, her dress creating the illusion of a leaf falling in the wind. As she fell, she swept her right arm forward and pointed her gun between Falk's startled eyes.

Falk, normally wary of a wounded antagonist, should have immediately flattened on the floor, but the excruciating pain in his chest refused to allow him. Instead, he continued staring helplessly down the distant muzzle of the foreign agent's gun, while clasping his left chest. In slow motion and with the hyper-acuity that typically accompanies imminent death, he watched the girl's index finger tighten about the trigger of her weapon, even while her body continued its loose fall to the floor.

Behind him, he heard Koski whisper, "Good enough to back you up," and was startled by two more loud reports from behind his left ear, followed by the familiar whizz of two bullets, each passing barely an inch away from the side of his head. A puff of smoke stung his eyes, briefly obscured his field of vision, and he felt his nose involuntarily wrinkle from the acrid smell of spent gunpowder. He knew there were loud sounds all about him, but the strength of the two reports had by now temporarily robbed him of his hearing on his left, leaving in its place an irritating buzz. Suddenly lightheaded, his vision, still focused tightly on the muzzle of the weapon pointed at him from the far side of the room, began narrowing. *All the cardinal signs of shock,* he thought before his head began to swirl and darkness overtake him.

From Falk's diminishing perspective, the two bullets fired from behind him sped, one immediately after the other in slow motion across the room, leaving what he saw or imagined were spiral wakes trailing behind.

The event was his last cohesive thought. Just before passing out, he thought he saw a momentary bright white light. Assuming he wasn't dying, at least not yet, that meant either the event had just occurred, or a bullet with his name on it was even now speeding on its way towards him. The terrifying thoughts, however, never completely formed. Falk was out cold.

Chapter 43

Falk woke in the arms of a woman.

He tried desperately to focus his blurry eyes, but lying on his back, staring up, all he could make out was a white-flocked popcorn ceiling, its tiny bright peaks and valley-shadows playing games with his mind, creating images of random objects, animals, places and faces from his past.

Faces.

His first cohesive thought was a question. *Where is Koski?* As his field of vision slowly expanded he noticed the face of the woman looking down at him. She was holding and rocking him. It was Kate Keenan, tears streaming down her cheeks, the tears splashing on his face. It was her tears, he realized, that had awakened him.

Kate was sitting cross-legged on the floor, cradling Falk's head, rocking and sobbing. Slowly he realized four other persons were peering down at him. Two were surprised-looking

289

fluorescent-orange-and-yellow-clothed EMS technicians. The other two were worried looking policemen.

The two EMS technicians dropped to their knees. "It's a miracle," voiced one to no one in particular. Kate paused in her rocking to look into Falk's eyes. He attempted a smile, but ended up cringing, an electric pain coursing from his left shoulder throughout his body.

"Oh my God! Oh my God, Falk! You're alive!" Kate voiced from above.

"Koski?" asked Falk, his voice weak and trembling from the searing pain. "Is she…alright?"

"Koski?" replied Kate. "Yes. I think so. She asked about you while they were taking her away."

One of the EMS technicians attempted without success to loosen Falk from Kate's embrace. "Ma'am. We need to look at his wound and get him to a hospital. Please…" The second technician slowly worked an arm between Kate's shoulder and the man she was so desperately clenching.

"Ma'am. Please let go," the first technician ordered, while his partner gently tugged the two apart.

"Falk?" Kate asked, the single word pregnant with meaning.

"Koski?" Falk replied, and fell back into unconsciousness.

When he next awoke, he was lying once again on his back

but this time on a moving stretcher, a plastic prong in each nostril hissing lightly, a bag of IV fluid swaying precariously above his right shoulder.

He felt better. The pain in his left shoulder was still there and, surprisingly, just as intense, but it seemed distant and unimportant. He felt as if he were floating rather than being whisked along on a litter. One of the two technicians was trotting beside him.

"Koski?" asked Falk, his mouth fighting him, feeling like it was filled with dry cotton. The technician bent over and gently probed his patient's neck and shoulder while they continued moving.

"Do…you…need…more…pain…medication?" he asked, as if talking to a recalcitrant child.

"Koski?" Falk asked again.

"The woman holding you when we arrived? She's okay. She left with some black-suited men. As far as we know, she sustained no injuries."

"Koski?" asked Falk again, more emphatically.

"The other woman? She's being treated at a nearby hospital. The same one where you're going."

"How…is…she?" Falk asked shakily, trying to keep away the blissful curtain of mist that seemed to want to close over him.

"She was...wounded. She's in surgery. Where you'll be going next."

"The...other...ones? The...girls?" he asked with increasing difficulty.

"The one we found in the room next to the table with the equipment was dead. The American in the bedroom was still alive when we arrived, and is also on her way to the hospital. She actually looked better than you..."

"I...I..." Falk stuttered, unable to formulate his next question, giving in at last to the medication.

Chapter 44

At Falk's next reawakening, he found himself tucked between crisp, white sheets, in what was clearly a hospital room. A uniformed guard was standing at attention at the inside door of what he assumed was a private room. Looking to his right, he was disappointed at not being able see outside through the expected window. Instead, a white curtain blocked his view.

Falk began moving fingers, toes, then hands, feet, arms and legs, noting the IV in the back of his right hand. *Okay,* he thought, *everything's still there*, until he attempted to move his chest. The resulting pain almost knocked him back out. *I must be better,* he thought acerbically, *they've stopped the morphine*, wincing again as he slowly moved his left shoulder.

While he was exploring the room and his body, a nurse entered with a tray of unappetizing liquid hospital food and several medications, each of which he was ordered to take.

Encouraging him to use his right arm and hand to drink, the

nurse silently surveyed her patient. The man in the bed facing her was handsome, in a rough and attractive way. Despite the extent of his injury, he appeared alert, cooperative and…well-muscled…again, in a rough and attractive way.

"Nurse?" he asked, breaking the silence, finishing what liquid he could after taking his medications. "I was told that I was brought to the hospital immediately after a woman-colleague of mine. Her name is Susan Koski. Can you tell me how she's doing?" Sensing the nurse's interest in him, he flashed a winning smile while giving his best impression of a lost puppy.

"I…well, we're not supposed to talk to patients about other patients, Mr. Falk, but I can say she survived surgery and, following discharge from the ICU, is recovering in the bed next to you. We don't usually accommodate two persons in a private room, but it was your superior's specific order. She's resting at the moment."

"Thank you," Falk offered with genuine joy. Koski was alright! He could wait to talk with her, as long as he knew she was alright!

The medications quickly made him feel sleepy, and the next time he awoke it was late afternoon. He knew this because the curtain separating him from Koski had been drawn back, and yellow-orange sunlight was streaming in obliquely through the window.

Koski was sitting up in bed, a turban bandage about her head.

"At last, our heroes awaken!" said Stewart gruffly from the foot of their beds. Beside him stood two uniformed officers. "This is Colonel Jack Rellin and this is General Richard Cavors," Stewart said pointing from one to the other. "Friends of mine. They're here to thank you."

Falk hardly heard what his boss was saying. He was trying to position himself to get a better look at Koski, who only had eyes for him.

"Ahem. You two can 'catch up' later. You'll have plenty of time recovering as you are, next to each other."

"How…how did you manage a room like this for…us? We're not formally married. I didn't know anyone knew of our personal feelings for each other."

"Affection isn't easy to conceal," Stewart replied.

Koski smiled, rolling what she had just heard around in her mind: not *formally* married. "I'm glad to hear your voice again, Falk. I thought…I thought you were…" she began.

"Like I said," Stewart interrupted, "you two will have plenty of time to catch up on everything over the next few days while you're here recovering. Right now, General Cavors and Colonel Rellin have something they want to share with you."

The general immediately stepped forward and cleared his throat. "I've been instructed by the Joint Chiefs of Staff on behalf of the President, the combined military forces and people of the United States of America, to formally thank you, Joseph Falk, and you, Susan Koski, as well as your partner, Kate Keenan, for stopping what appeared to be collapse of the United States of America, and doing so at great personal risk."

Falk, lacking the details, could do little more than nod.

Koski glanced from Falk to the two officers then back at Falk, looking momentarily flattered, and offered the same simple nod.

General Cavors, at a loss for further words, cleared his throat again and stepped back.

"You also have the thanks of the National Security Agency and the combined security services of the United States of America and her allies. On all our behalves, I offer you our collective, and my personal thanks," Colonel Rellin added.

Koski and Falk acknowledged the thanks with a simple "Your welcome" and confused, guilty-looking smiles.

"There are many others wanting to thank you three. From individual Americans to heads of state. It's been difficult maintaining your and our organization's anonymity given the magnitude of what you three accomplished," Stewart added, looking anxiously at his watch. "But more of that later. Colonel

Rellin and General Cavors are on strict schedules. I'll remain for a few more minutes to answer any pressing questions. The hospital is very strict about visiting hours."

The two military men saluted Koski and Falk, then turned on heel and exited, striking up a conversation on their way out of the room. The guard at the door clicked his heels and stood stiffly, opening the door and offering a salute as they passed.

"What exactly happened?" asked Falk, after the door closed behind the two men.

"A few minutes isn't time enough to go into the details, but suffice it to say that your mission to Hawaii to capture an agent and handler was successful."

"Really?" asked Falk sincerely. "I thought the Oriental girl died."

"Yes, well, that's an interesting story in and of itself. She did, but the American, you see, survived, and provided us with enough information to locate and capture their handler. We're currently interrogating each separately, but on threat of returning him to North Korea, the handler gladly offered us everything he knew, and we have the girl to corroborate it."

"The other girl was a professional's professional," said Falk in a hushed voice. "Why didn't she dispose of her American partner like she did their American homestay parent?"

"Like I said," Stewart replied. "'Affection isn't easy to

conceal'. Apparently the two had formed a more than collegial bond, and when it came time for the North Korean agent to kill her American friend, she wavered, her first shot wounding her in the neck, her second more hurried shot striking her girlfriend in the thigh. With all the blood from the two hits, it's easy to imagine the killer assuming that her partner was mortally wounded. As you said, she was a professional's professional, but for just a moment, it looks like she let her feelings for her American girlfriend get in the way."

"And the event?" Koski and Falk asked together, exchanging a look and smile at the unusual synchronicity of their questions.

"Ah, yes. The 'endgame event', for that's what it was. It never happened. It *should* have, but the black box you tossed into the room did its job. Kate was *mostly* certain it would, but I have to admit that, at the time, the rest of us didn't share her confidence.

"According to her, the laws of quantum mechanics do not allow two of exactly the same objects to continue existing. Kate's black box—I'll let her explain the technical details surrounding it—was designed to react to two situations: First, if it were present during the moment of quantum entanglement, it would assume precedence, appear simultaneously at both locations, and remain after the entanglement ended at the second site. Second, as soon as the entanglement resolved, it delivered what Kate is calling her 'gift that couldn't be refused'. Again, I'll let her fill in the technical details. She'll be coming by later when she can wrangle some time away from the NSA folks, who are falling over her to find out how exactly her device works."

"What of the auctions?" Kate, sitting up straighter, asked.

"Some thought they were a red herring, but I always suspected they were more," Stewart replied. "As it turns out, they were a key part of the overall endgame, but I'll let David, Lou and Kate fill you in on that. They would feel sorely affronted if I stole their thunder. They'll have an opportunity later to congratulate you in person and recount their part in ending the auctions.

"Kate, by the way, played no small part in it all," continued Stewart. "While she was busy concocting her 'gift' to send back to the folks at Pyongyang, she was also acting as devil's advocate to the NSA computer geeks. Her foil, in addition to what we obtained from our mole in Bureau 121, was exactly what was needed to allow David, Lou and the NSA to track the fifth auction through the dark TOR internet and definitively locate both seller and buyers. It was also Kate's genius that gave the NSA folks a way to end the auctions in our favor. But, again, my time is limited, and those are stories I'm certain

David, Lou and Kate would rather tell you themselves."

Falk shifted his weight slightly in his bed, wincing uncomfortably, and nodded his agreement. In the next bed, Koski's smile turned to the semblance of a frown. It wasn't that she couldn't bear to see her lover in pain. She'd seen that before and would undoubtedly see it again. No, it was that the showdown for the world had ended, and it was now time for her more difficult woman-to-woman showdown with Kate.

Chapter 45

As promised, David Hallard, Cerebrus Head of Field Operations, and Lou Richards, Head of External Security, dropped by just before evening.

"We tried to get here sooner, but things at Cerebrus are pretty crazy right now. How are the two of you doing?" asked David.

"Okay," Koski and Falk replied together and laughed.

"Okay," Falk repeated. "We're both okay. So tell us what happened with the auction," he urged.

Hallard and Richards looked at each other. Richards nodded to Hallard, so Hallard began.

"First, I've got to say that the 'Tiger Team' exercise proved...prophctic. You know about it, right? Stewart told you about it?"

"No," Koski and Falk answered again together.

"Well, that isn't really surprising. A lot was going on just then," Hallard reported. "Stewart heard from his contacts that the Joint Chiefs were seriously considering a pre-emptive strike against Russia, assuming that Russia was attempting to humiliate and destroy the USA in a manner similar to that which they experienced during *perestroika* and *glasnost.*

"Stewart called a 'Tiger Team' and used the Delphi Technique to force consensus among us where, truthfully, none existed. The result was unanimous agreement that Russia couldn't be directly behind either the events or the auctions. Given the evidence, it had to be North Korea. We found out later, through you and Kate, that Russia had been developing a prototype device which they were field testing with the help of the Chinese. The Russians called it a *kvantovaya mashina smerti*—a 'Quantum Death Machine'."

Hallard paused to take a breath and Richards took over. "So, you see, in essence, both were right in regard to the events, but each only partially so. The auction, on the other hand, while clearly a correlated phenomenon, had a different 'feel' to it. Our 'Tiger Team' came to consensus that the auctions must be almost entirely North Korean, primarily, we surmised for economic reasons. In short, the money received from the 'sale' of regions of the USA was used to, first, have the USA fund its own demise—more about that later—and second, to secure North Korea economically. Clever way to get around all the sanctions, if I do say so. With enough money, they could solve their 'quality-of life' problems, impress the citizenry with their ability to rule, and obtain the weaponry needed for full-scale theater warfare. They could buy anything they needed. Rags to riches in one swoop."

"They had the means and desire," continued Hallard. "The only thing they lacked was the mechanism, and that proved to be the BitCoin auctions. BitCoins were the perfect medium: Untraceable, they could be used directly or exchanged into any currency, their value only increasing with time and demand, and the mechanism was already in place worldwide. It remained only for them to locate and convince potential 'bidders' that what they were 'selling' was 'real'. That's where the events and auctions operated symbiotically. The challenge for us was to figure out a way to stop the combined processes before it was too late."

"And it almost proved so," Richards picked up excitedly. The two were obviously enjoying relating their stories Tweedle Dee and Tweedle Dum style to their captive audience. "By the second auction, we had already begun participating in bidding for our own regions. It was Kate Keenan's idea to tag some 'return receipt' code packets onto our 'bid'. It required two more auction 'return receipts', and final confirmation by our mole in Bureau 121 to feel confident that we'd identified the electronic pathway. Once we confirmed it was North Korea and knew the bid pathway, we set about identifying the bidders. In the end, we needed the Hawaii auction to conclusively track and identify all of them, but, of course, by that time, it could have ended up an academic exercise as the USA should have functionally ceased to exist. Just before the Hawaii event, NSA convinced the electronic security forces of our allies to join us in aggressively seizing control of the entire dark TOR network and all BitCoin exchanges. Stewart came up with the idea that after the successful bidder had sent his money, we would flood the market with our own secret stash of BitCoins, effectively driving their value down to near nothing, leaving all the auction participants holding massive debts, in many cases larger than their net worth."

"It was a big gamble," Hallard said, taking over again from Richards. "In fact, we went dangerously beyond 'breaking the bank' in order to participate in the auctions. Luckily we 'owned' the value of the BitCoins, having begun aggressively mining them immediately after the first auction, in an ultimately failed attempt to break the block encryption and identify the participants that way."

"This has got to be one of the most complex terrorist attacks yet," Falk interjected.

"Seems more like a brutal act of war," summed up Koski.

"Ah, but technically, it wasn't either," said Richards. "That's the beauty of it upon looking back. 'Terrorist attacks' are defined as non-state attacks, and 'acts of war' as involving the use of physical force. Neither technically occurred, though the Joint Chiefs were ready to characterize what was happening as an 'act of cyberwar' and actually instigate a global military response. It doesn't even fit the definition of 'cyber espionage', as, if you think about it, nothing was ever actually stolen. The closest anyone came to naming what we have just experienced is 'organized hacking' and even that's flimsy at best given the extent of it."

"So we're entering a new age of conflict," Falk ventured. "One more insidious than ever before. Just when the United Nations was making inroads against war by agreeing to hold leaders of the attacking nations personally responsible for the suffering and loss of life, and the aggressor nation for not only the direct expenses of the war, but for the cost of both aggressor and defender population's physical and mental 'recovery' to pre-war levels. Just then, along comes this incident to blur everything."

"So North Korea starts a world war and gets off Scot-free?" inquired Koski.

"Not entirely so, but that's Kate's story to tell," Hallard added cryptically. "She's been in debriefings all day, but she told us to tell you that she would be visiting as soon as she could break away, perhaps later tonight or tomorrow."

"Brilliant woman, that Kate," concluded Rogers, gathering up his coat and hat, and preparing to leave.

'*A truly brilliant woman*', thought Koski with a mixture of awe and antipathy.

Chapter 46

"Bandage changes before dinner!" the physician's assistant announced with a cheerfulness that neither Falk nor Koski shared. "Think of it as an appetizer." he added with a smirk.

For Koski, the bandage change was quick and mostly painless: Unwrap the old head bandage, remove the gauze pad, check the ten or so wicked-looking scalp sutures that would one day be hidden beneath her hair, place on a new gauze pad, and rewrap. She would need to remain in the hospital, the physician's assistant advised, at least for another day of observation before being free to leave.

For Falk, it was a different matter entirely. After his left arm sling was carefully removed, the shoulder bandages needed to be unwrapped. During this time, even the slightest arm movement, actively or passively, resulted in a flurry of gut-wrenching pain, reminding him of how he felt just after being shot. Tossing the black box into the room had proven almost unbearable. It was pure luck that he was able to toss it at all.

In actuality, Falk was more than lucky. The bullet had struck and bounced off his left collarbone, leaving it shattered. A higher caliber bullet would have penetrated through and likely punctured his lung. Half an inch lower and major arteries, veins and nerves would have been shredded. The surgeons had repositioned the two broken ends, inserted a temporary rod and packed in bone chips from elsewhere in his body then sewn him back up leaving a nasty-looking, four-inch long, gross looking, black-sutured gash. Looking at the heavily bruised wound in the mirror during the dressing change, it left him feeling like he was part Frankenstein monster. It would be at least a week before they would issue a final prognosis and, then, a carefully planned, rigorous, only slightly less painful physical therapy regime awaited him in order to keep his muscles from weakening during his anticipated three-to-four-month convalescence.

As the physician's assistant with the help of the private duty nurse wetted and removed the gauze pad, Falk held his breath and gritted his teeth. The PA picked and prodded, finally declaring the wound to be, "Looking good."

Falk tried to turn his head left to see directly for himself, but the pain was too much, and he ended up easing his body carefully back in the bed.

"It is," a familiar voice offered from the bed next to his. Falk turned carefully to his right towards the two alluring eyes peering at him from beneath what looked like an Arabian turban.

It thankfully proved much less painful to turn his head toward Koski. "Thanks, Koski. I needed to hear that. With medical people, 'looking good' can mean almost anything."

The alluring eyes blinked and Falk imagined them looking warmly and lovingly at him while the two made passionate love. *It will be awhile before that fantasy becomes…* he began thinking, sadly interrupting the thought. But at least they were both alive, intact, and, with time, would resume their work and relationship.

When the gauze pad over his stitches had been replaced with an "ouch-less" non-stick pad, the area re-bandaged, and the arm returned to its protective sling, Falk let out a long sigh and relaxed. The physician's assistant and nurse were quickly replaced by a passable hospital meal.

Late the next night, a frazzled Kate Keenan knocked at Koski and Falk's hospital door. Their twenty-four-hour guard cracked open the door, and after some discussion admitted her. Kate walked soberly, hands behind her back, to halfway between the foots of their beds, looked long at Falk, briefly at

Koski and back at Falk.

"I…I…" she began as if unsure what to say, swinging her right hand forward and presenting a bright flower bouquet to both and neither. Falk smiled. Koski stiffened. Kate continued to direct the bouquet between Falk and Koski's beds, drifting slowly towards Falk's.

An awkward silence ensued, which, Falk noted quizzically, was quite unlike Kate. Once again, he sensed something happening onto which he couldn't quite put his finger. He was about to voice a prefunctory "Thank you" when Koski spoke.

"Thank you, Kate," she said. "They're lovely. You can put them on my tray-table if you like. I'll call the nurse to place them in a vase." Koski nodded towards her hospital bed tray located between her and Falk.

Falk watched Kate closely. To him, she looked tired, haggard, and…what? Contrite? Kate's posture softened and her initially enigmatic Mona-Lisa-like smile was replaced with one of genuine caring. Something was being communicated between the two women, that was obvious, but exactly what continued to escaped him.

A moment later the nurse entered, and, at Koski's request, selected a plastic water jug in which she gathered and arranged the flowers. Finished, she held flowers out to Koski as if for approval.

"Please put them on the cabinet between us," Koski said, indicating with her finger the metal cabinet located against the wall equal-distance between her and Falk's bed. To Falk, her voice seemed more determined than usual. The nurse complied and, looking quickly from one woman to the other, quietly took her leave. As the nurse left, Falk thought he saw both women relax.

"Susan, I think I owe you an…"

"No, Kate. It's *you* to whom *I* owe the apology," Koski cut in, the tone of her voice firm but contrite and acquiescent.

"No, Susan, I…"

"What the hell's going on?" Falk interrupted, truly puzzled by what he was hearing and seeing. "Is this some kind of new field code?"

Both women stared at Falk, then at each other as if gauging the other's mettle, then both broke out in laughter.

"Girl stuff," replied Kate Keenan, wiping her eyes and resuming her bearing, having been appointed in reward for her actions a department rather than a division and with it a massive new set of "toys," as well as an entirely new perspective on Cerebrus' mission.

"'Girl stuff,'" repeated Koski, looking over at Falk and extending a hand towards him.

Falk stretched awkwardly and, in the end, painfully, to

touch her fingertips, before wincing and pulling his hand back.

Kate watched the two, her face belying no further feeling or emotion. "I came here to thank you both: Joe for supporting me in the field during a time of…well…personal crisis, and you, Susan, for saving me and later Joe on the stairway. I realize now that I'm not meant to be a field agent. That's for you and Joe…together…as the incredible team you've always been. I am indebted to you both."

"Thanks, Kate. I appreciate you telling me that," Koski replied. "But in the field, we don't carry debts. Covering each other is our job. You owe us nothing but your continued friendship."

"What Susan just said is true," Falk added, feeling more of an intruder than a participant in the conversation, but wanting greatly to be included, though why, exactly, he wasn't sure.

"I'm here to answer any questions you might have about what happened after you tossed the box into the room just before the event."

"I have several questions," replied Falk. "But first, I think both Susan and I owe you our thanks for not just apparently saving the United States of America, but also saving…us. Exactly how you did it, I'm still not clear, but you ended up playing the principle role in this whole operation, and playing it with an undeniably level head and cool expertise. To you go my personal congratulations, though I would guess they'll be lost in those from every American from the President on down."

Kate blushed. "Thank you, Joe," she said, rather coolly he thought. Turning to Koski, Kate continued, "That's some man you have there."

"I know," replied Koski emphatically, directing another smile at Falk.

Despite all his effort, Falk again felt the outsider in the conversation. There was clearly a purpose behind what the two women were indirectly saying to each other. About one thing, however, he felt certain: Something unsettling was going on right in front of him. When earlier, Kate had blushed, he had felt…what?…warmness? A protectiveness that he hadn't truly felt before? The feeling, however, disappeared during their discussion as rapidly as it had appeared.

"I'm sure you're wondering about the little 'gift' to the North Koreans," Kate continued in business-like voice. "If you recall, Joe, in Operation Finding Kate, I developed a process where screenwriters could dictate a screenplay, and instead of it resulting in a computer-generated script, it recreated actual audio-visual characters. Robotic characters so realistic that viewers would mistake them for live human actors. Taken together, one could 'dictate' a believable movie. Not entirely, but enough so that the techies could, with say, an hour's additional labor, edit and polish it to the point that it was ready for viewing in theaters. That was what got me into the situation in which you found me and from which afterwards you 'rescued' me.

"At your recommendation, Joe, I was offered and accepted an ultra-secret job within Cerebrus. Initially, no division or department, just me, an amazing laboratory, and unlimited funding to continue developing the technology I'd invented. What we sent back to the Koreans was the result of years of research and development. The scary part for me was that it was also my lab's first full-scale *weaponized* field deployment. I was *pretty* certain it would work, having tested and retested all its various components. We had to put them together into a less than a few centimeter sized "black box" which we tested as best we could in the field under carefully controlled conditions, but never in an actual situation like this. "

"All that must have weighed heavily on you when you joined me in the room with the wounded girl and relinquished the box to save her life," Falk said, choosing his words carefully and watching the two women for their reaction.

Koski said nothing. Her look of respect said it for her.

"Yes," Kate replied simply. "At that moment, I felt…well, I felt mostly…confused. A lot *was* weighing heavily on my…

mind." Falk noticed Kate's face flush momentarily. "Yes, well, the little black box: What we conjured up was an inductive pulse device that, instead of exploding or creating a 'big bang' in *their* room, created a much bigger bang in their minds. Basically, a number of selected, integrated-wave-pulses were produced that stimulate portions of the brain that cause the recipients to see whatever they want to see. Not just 'want', but need, wish or desire to see. And not just 'see' but actually *believe*. It's different from the 'events', in that the pulses from my device diminish slower as they travel outwards.

"The initial effect on those closest would be confusion. You see, those slightly further away would be momentarily *unaffected,* leaving them trying to make sense out of what the effected were saying and doing, the effect slowly rippling it's way outward."

Koski and Falk looked puzzled.

"For example," Kate clarified, "if a North Korean working on the project desperately wanted the event to be successful, maybe for fear of his, her or a family member's life, that person would immediately interpret all sensory information—sight, sound, smell, taste, touch—into the seemingly 'real' experience that the event actually *had* been successful. For that person, in fact, their effort would have been *wildly* successful, while at the same time equally frightening in that they would feel that they would likely never be able to be this successful on any subsequent project. To the affected individual, the combination of relief and new-found fear would be absolutely real. Likewise, an as yet unaffected nearby observer would be thrown into a sense of profound disorientation, knowing the project had failed, despite the opposite behavior of those affected, even more so, knowing that their effort had backfired in some very strange way they weren't able to comprehend."

Kate paused to let the two agents take in what she'd shared.

"My God!" Falk exclaimed.

Koski's expression slowly turned to one of compassion. She was only now beginning to appreciate the immense pressure that Kate must have been working under. Preparing to deploy a singular device, the results of which she was uncertain, in the field, weapon in hand, she would have desperately needed someone to share her burden with. Someone like Falk.

"Yes. 'My God!' That's exactly what kept running through my mind, even as I handed you the device to deploy for me. 'My God, what am I doing? What am I unleashing?' I felt like Oppenheimer, when in a flash, his work was transformed from the greatest gift that humankind had ever been given into the most destructive device ever known. A device far beyond the moral capacity of anyone to understand and, more so, control."

"Wouldn't the effects be limited to those in the room?"

Koski asked.

"And why, in the end, didn't we experience the fifth event?" Falk added.

"Both good questions," replied Kate. "I said I had my research group busy preparing the device, but in actuality, they were modifying it in three key ways: According to the laws of quantum mechanics, an object and its 'clone' can only co-exist while quantum-entangled, a state that is so short and ephemeral, we have yet to be able to measure it with any real precision. Call it the 'present' if you wish. The entanglement exists only in the 'present moment', sandwiched between past and future. Once the present moment is over, the quantum entanglement ceases and the paradox of two of the same thing co-existing at the same time in two different places has to resolve. Either it remains at the site of origin, or it remains at the target site. That being said, what ended up in North Korea, wasn't the little black box."

"Huh?" replied Falk. "Then what was sent?"

"The *result* of the device being activated in a quantum-entanglement condition. What was transmitted back to the North Koreans was the *result* of the activated device: a plasma wave packet that experientially altered their minds. Nothing more, nothing less. And, the second trait I asked my scientists to incorporate into our little gift used the same physics that caused the North Korean events to echo and expand. In our case, the 'event' the North Koreans experienced will slowly spread, affecting the same change in anyone through whom the echo passes. Everyone, we think, within several hundred miles of the epicenter. The third trait proved most difficult to engineer but is also the most interesting: Anyone on the other end of any electrical or electronic connection to the epicenter, say, talking on a telephone line, radiotelephone or cell phone…"

"That means the North Korean leadership…" began Koski, astounded at what she was hearing.

"Yes. At this very moment they all 'see' the world as they need, want or desire it to be. Franklin, David, Albert, and Lou have been busy these past hours manipulating world news so that the combination of the news and the perceptions of the affected will slowly chisel out a new 'reality' for them, one where the attitudes and behavior of current North Korean leaders will be altered, hopefully for the better. Remember, we didn't have time to fully test the results of the completed weapon.

"As for our not experiencing *their* 'endgame event', the answer is really quite simple: Mathematically speaking, two entanglements can't co-exist at the same moment in the same space-time. One or the other entangled pair must *never have*

318

existed. My technicians made certain our gift would have a slightly more powerful 'kick' during quantum entanglement than their space-time tear. In short, their endgame event not only didn't happen, *it never existed at all.* If that still seems paradoxical, remember that entanglements can only exist in the true present moment. Whatever ceases to exist in the present moment cannot become past. And because of this, there will be no trace of who or what caused it, or that it ever happened."

"And you accomplished all this between the fourth and fifth events?" asked Falk, overawed in turn.

"Not really. I developed the theoretical foundations during my time with Cerebrus. I had to trust my dedicated crew of Cerebrus research scientists to bring everything quickly to fruition. I imagine the full impact of what we've accomplished hasn't yet begun to sink in. The old Einstein-Oppenheimer effect: By unleashing this new 'weapon', the world as we knew it before has been replaced by one in which quantum entanglement will now play a major role. There's no going back. And the ethical considerations, I suspect, will prove even more challenging than the advent of the atomic age. I don't know whether to smile or cry." Indeed, Kate's eyes were misting as she spoke.

"So, in the end, all our our efforts to capture the two agents and their handler made no real difference after all," observed

Falk glumly.

"Oh, quite the contrary," replied Kate with what could only be called a look of love. "The Oriental agent's former 'friend', and to an even greater extent, her handler were quite willing to share everything they knew about the workings of the interconnected receivers, which gave our side a point of reference to compare my effort to. Half of any battle is always in the understanding. Hearing what they shared made my seemingly unbelievable explanation all the more believable. Your sacrifices were hardly in vain. Without you two, our future would have likely been quite different. Instead, there's a world outside this room waiting to thank you. True, the thanks will be filtered through Cerebrus in order to preserve your anonymity and allow you to continue your work. My 'thanks' are my promotion, and with it, even more secrecy and anonymity. Aside from Stewart and you two, I doubt anyone will soon know I did anything or ever existed."

A long silence hung heavily in the air between Kate and the two agents.

"Thank you, Kate," Koski replied softly on both her and Falk's behalf but on two quite different levels,. "Thank you from the bottom of both our hearts."

Epilogue

Koski and Falk walked together, his better right hand grasping Koski's left, along the tree-lined south side of the Reflection Pool of the Washington Mall. By all rights, the night should have been pitch black given the blanket of low-lying clouds above, but a soft side light, emanating as if by magic from the illuminated trees, coupled with the blaze of the Washington Monument behind them and the Lincoln Memorial ahead imparted a truly romantic glow.

Koski hadn't noticed. She was busy studying the face of the man she loved. It was a different face from the one she remembered prior to this mission. Beneath its weathered exterior had always existed a boy's rakish smile; a Peter Pan to her Wendy. Tonight, however, Falk's face looked tense. Faint lines showed in the corners of his eyes and mouth, a residual, she assumed, from the constant pain he'd suffered during the last four months. Getting back in shape after the collarbone fracture had proven more difficult than either had thought. Just when he was starting to feel better, the surgeons brought him back into the hospital to remove the pin, sending him back to where he'd been the night he woke in the hospital after...

It was clear to Koski that Falk was lost in thought. Painful ones. She placed an arm around his waist as they walked together, leaned her head against his good shoulder and smiled up at him.

Falk cringed momentarily, a reflex he'd acquired during the four months of "torture," as he sometimes called it. As an agent, he'd been trained to steel himself against such, but his recovery, stretching out as long as it had, had taken its toll, leaving him physically and mentally exhausted.

"'A penny for your thoughts'," Koski, stretching to her full height, whispered in his ear.

Falk stopped and turned to face the water, Koski positioned between. "I was thinking back to the hallway of that house," Falk replied. "Twice, I didn't know if you were alive or dead. For a while, I didn't know if *I* was alive or dead. I didn't know if we would ever be together again. In truth, I was forced to face our deaths, individually and together."

"Everything happened so fast. For a moment, *I* didn't know if you were dead or alive, but here we are, together, walking our favorite walk, with all that behind us and a whole new world ahead."

"For a moment, I found myself mourning your passing," Falk whispered in anguish.

"Oh, Joe! I can't begin to imagine what you were feeling back there, and frankly I don't want to remember how I felt, but we're here. Now. Together."

"Yes," replied Falk, shaking off the agony the incident and his slow recovery for the umpteenth time. "It was the first time I truly felt my mortality. I don't want to lose you, Susan. The doctor's say I'm fit for duty, and I'm ready to serve, but I don't ever again want to lose you."

"You needn't worry about that," Susan Koski replied. "Oh, and by the way, I have a belated birthday gift for you," she added, and touched her lips to his.

Joseph Falk slipped both his hands around her waist, and held her tightly against him in a lover's embrace.

No, each thought. *I needn't worry about that ever again. At least, not for tonight.*

If you enjoyed *Quantum Death* consider the first book in the Koski and Falk series, *Who's Killing All the Lawyers?*

Lawyers are being murdered by laser-driven arrows. The FBI believes that someone is training a Native American militia to take over the economic system in the U.S. Joe Falk and Susan Koski are assigned to find the hired killer and The Fox, the real force behind the killings.

GREAT SOUTHWEST BOOK FESTIVAL AWARD
AMAZON KINDLE GENRE BESTSELLER

...the second in the Koski and Falk series, *The Judas List:*

Between the end of World War II and the winter of 1975, a 700-year-old prayer book, a key and a faded blueprint came to light in Vienna, and began a 25-year search for Nazi Herman Goering's treasure. In modern day Vienna, American agents Koski and Falk must go undercover to locate the treasure and the Judas List—a compendium of individuals and organizations that financed WWII, and, in it's aftermath, now intended to manipulate world finances to bring about the Fourth Reich. But the Americans aren't the only ones looking for the list and the treasure. So are ex-Nazi, the Bosnians, Russians and, most recently, Muslim militants.

PACIFIC RIM BOOK FESTIVAL AWARD

...the third book in the Falk and Koski adventure series, *Imminent Danger* by A. G. Hayes.

Jamul, an adored American pop singer, dreams of a grand show of Islamic Jihad power, intending to use a biological weapon to eradicate religious leaders at an Easter service at the Hollywood Bowl. In response, Cerberus agents Joe Falk and Susan Koski must seek help from unlikely sources-gang bangers, scientists and the public-to stop the next brutal terrorist attack on American soil.

LA BOOK FESTIVAL AWARD

…and the fourth in the multi-award-winning Koski and Falk series, *The Chemical Factor*:

A stolen weapon of mass destruction hidden years ago on board the Queen Mary, has remained there unknown and undisturbed. That is, up to now. Agents Falk and Koski are called in to evacuate the ship and somehow locate the bomb. Running out of time, they risk their lives to locate the weapon, not knowing that a Girl Scout strayed from her group during evacuation and is hiding in the ship's Trafalgar Square gift shop.

About the Authors

A. G. Hayes studied television writing at UCLA. He has published short fiction, including *Cover Up*, *Not a Penny Pincher*, *Home*, *Payment in Full*, *Small Wonder* and *Guided through a Mine Field*, and written scripts for CBS TV and other television production companies. He lives in the Sierra Nevada Foothills and spends his time writing and traveling to nearly every part of the world. He has used personal experiences gained during service with the British intelligence in Eastern Europe and the Middle East to enrich the characters of his protagonist teams. He is the multi-award-winning author of *Who's Killing All the Lawyers* (Savant 2011), *The Judas List* (Savant 2012), *Imminent Danger* (Savant 2013) and *The Chemical Factor* (Savant 2015).

Raymond Gaynor is the pen-name of a multi-award-winning,
reclusive writer-artist-photographer-videographer, who, in his own
words, "lives and breathes" San Francisco. He co-authored with
William Maltese on the Tripler and Clarke gay political thriller, *Total
Meltdown* (Borgo/Wildside 2011) and is the author of numerous
fiction and non-fiction works published under a number of
pseudonyms.

If you enjoyed *Quantum Death,* consider these other fine books from Savant Books and Publications:

Essay, Essay, Essay by Yasuo Kobachi
Aloha from Coffee Island by Walter Miyanari
Footprints, Smiles and Little White Lies by Daniel S. Janik
The Illustrated Middle Earth by Daniel S. Janik
Last and Final Harvest by Daniel S. Janik
A Whale's Tale by Daniel S. Janik
Tropic of California by R. Page Kaufman
Tropic of California (the companion music CD) by R. Page Kaufman
The Village Curtain by Tony Tame
Dare to Love in Oz by William Maltese
The Interzone by Tatsuyuki Kobayashi
Today I Am a Man by Larry Rodness
The Bahrain Conspiracy by Bentley Gates
Called Home by Gloria Schumann
Kanaka Blues by Mike Farris
First Breath edited by Z. M. Oliver
Poor Rich by Jean Blasiar
Ammon's Horn by Guerrino Amati
The Jumper Chronicles by W. C. Peever
William Maltese's Flicker by William Maltese
My Unborn Child by Orest Stocco
Last Song of the Whales by Four Arrows
Perilous Panacea by Ronald Klueh
Falling but Fulfilled by Zachary M. Oliver
Mythical Voyage by Robin Ymer
Hello, Norma Jean by Sue Dolleris
Richer by Jean Blasiar
Manifest Intent by Mike Farris
Charlie No Face by David B. Seaburn
Number One Bestseller by Brian Morley
My Two Wives and Three Husbands by S. Stanley Gordon
In Dire Straits by Jim Currie
Wretched Land by Mila Komarnisky
Chan Kim by Ilan Herman
Who's Killing All the Lawyers? by A. G. Hayes
Ammon's Horn by G. Amati
Wavelengths edited by Zachary M. Oliver
Almost Paradise by Laurie Hanan
Communion by Jean Blasiar and Jonathan Marcantoni
The Oil Man by Leon Puissegur
Random Views of Asia from the Mid-Pacific by William E. Sharp

The Isla Vista Crucible by Reilly Ridgell
Blood Money by Scott Mastro
In the Himalayan Nights by Anoop Chandola
On My Behalf by Helen Doan
Traveler's Rest by Jonathan Marcantoni
Keys in the River by Tendai Mwanaka
Chimney Bluffs by David B. Seaburn
The Loons by Sue Dolleris
Light Surfer by David Allan Williams
The Judas List by A. G. Hayes
Path of the Templar - Book 2 of The Jumper Chronicles by W. C. Peever
The Desperate Cycle by Tony Tame
Shutterbug by Buz Sawyer
Blessed are the Peacekeepers by Tom Donnelly/Mike Munger
Purple Haze by George B. Hudson
The Turtle Dances by Daniel S. Janik
The Lazarus Conspiracies by Richard Rose
Imminent Danger by A. G. Hayes
Lullaby Moon by Malia Elliott of Leon & Malia
Volutions edited by Suzanne Langford
In the Eyes of the Son by Hans Brinckmann
The Hanging of Dr. Hanson by Bentley Gates
Written in the Stars - An Anthology edited by Sabrina Favors
Elaine of Corbenic by Tima Z. Newman
Ballerina Birdies by Marina Yamamoto
More, More Time by David Seaburn
Crazy Like Me by Erin Lee
Cleopatra Unconquered by Helen R. Davis
Valedictory by Daniel Scott
The Chemical Factor by A. G. Hayes

Coming Works
Running From the Pack edited by Helen R. Davis
Big Heaven by Charlotte Hebert
All Things Await by Seth Clabough
Captain Riddle's Treasure by GV Rama Rao
Libido Tsunami by Cate Burns
The Adventures of Purple Head, Buddha Monkey Sticky Feet by Erik Bracht
Cereus by Z. Roux
In the Shadows of My Mind by Andrew Massie

http://www.savantbooksandpublications.com